UNDER THE VIADUCT

H. L. ANDERSON

Immortal Works LLC
1505 Glenrose Drive
Salt Lake City, Utah 84104
Tel: (385) 202-0116

Cover Art by Megan King and Ashley Literski
www.approximatelymeganndesign.com
http://strangedevotion.wixsite.com/strangedesigns

ISBN 978-1-953491-15-2 (Paperback)
ASIN B08YN87M48 (Kindle Edition)

"To Wayne and Kilee: The boy who was saved and the girl who saved him.

And to my husband, Steve: You're my favorite human."

CHAPTER 1

Ash and bits of burning paper spiraled above the metal barrel as the wind picked up. Kaylee hid in the shadows a half-block away from the ragged group surrounding the fire beneath the viaduct, their hands held above the flames licking from the rim. She squinted, trying to determine if this was the group she'd been looking for.

A man with a dark brown tangled beard looked up at her just in time for their eyes to meet. She held her breath for a few heartbeats, worried about the danger she'd put herself in alone in this part of town—a Denver she never knew existed. The man tilted his head to the side in a quick show of curiosity, then returned his gaze to the hypnotics of the flames. Kaylee blew out her breath, the warm air mixing with the frigid to form a puff of white.

Quick footsteps sounded behind her. She twisted at the waist, and with no time for fight or flight to kick in, was met by a man, still running, as he tackled her to the ground. With a grunt, every ounce of air in her lungs whooshed out as she hit the gravel. Her phone flew from her hand, landing with a crunch several feet out of her reach. She couldn't even draw in a breath, much less scream for help, not that she expected any to come.

She punched her assailant's face, scratching at his eyes as her own vision became spotty before her. Her legs pinned under the weight of the brown-toothed man, she couldn't even kick him. He got a grip on her wrists and leaned down to push them against the ground, his face so close to hers their noses nearly touched—just as her lungs decided to start working again. She breathed in his rancid breath—all rot-gut whiskey, rotting teeth, and recently smoked... something. Meth, maybe? She had no idea what meth smelled like, but if she had to guess, this was it.

She retched, fear and disgust causing her whole body to tremble as she tried to hold in the street tacos she'd wolfed down a couple hours ago. Her head wasn't clearing up as quickly as it should now that she was getting oxygen. And it hurt. The back of her head hurt. She'd been concentrating so hard on re-inflating her lungs, she'd missed the fact that her head had bounced off a rock or something else solid.

"Heh. Yer a perty one," her attacker slurred. He released her right hand to paw at the zipper of her coat. "See what's under there..."

Twisting away from his groping hand, she screamed and raked the side of his face with her fingernails. It wasn't as effective as she'd hoped it would be, she'd bitten her nails down to the quick during mid-terms last week. Kaylee squeezed her eyes shut as the man raised his hand in a fist.

The blow glanced off her temple, adding to the swimming in her head. Her eyes flew open as his weight shifted. The man she'd made eye contact with above the flames of the barrel slammed into her assailant, rolling her to her side with the force of his attack.

Kaylee covered her head with her arms to keep the men's flailing feet from connecting with her already-damaged head and curled into a ball. Gravel crunched beneath them for a few seconds before a new voice—not the voice of her attacker—said, "Get out of here. And don't come back."

A gentle touch to her arm. Kaylee twitched and squeezed her eyes shut tighter.

"Are you okay?" His quiet voice surprised her with its softness. Shouldn't homeless people have rough voices to match their countenance?

She slowly removed her arms from around her head and uncurled from her fetal position. Shadowed eyes stared at her from beneath dirty bangs pressed flat by a blue and orange beanie. "I...I think so." She pushed herself up to a sitting position. Mistake. The world spun about her as her vision faded around the edges. "Oh..." She lowered herself back to the cold ground.

"You're not okay," the man mumbled. "Do you have a phone? I think I should call an ambulance."

"No. No ambulance. Just give me a minute." She touched the center point of pain on the back of her head—her fingers came away wet and sticky. She opened her eyes, trying to focus on her fingers as she held them in front of her face.

"You're bleeding. And shivering."

"I'm okay." She just needed to find her phone and get back to her car. Alone. Her teeth chattered. She pushed up on her elbow, slower this time, and searched the ground.

"Look," he swiped the hair out of his downcast eyes, "you should at least let me take a look at that cut on your head and let me help you to the fire so you can get warm while you recover a little."

"My phone." She'd finally spotted it a few yards away. She shoved herself up, intending to stand so she could go get it. "Whoa," she covered her mouth with her hands as she sunk back down to her side, "I'm gonna throw up."

The man retrieved her phone then knelt beside her while she took quick breaths, trying to keep the nausea at bay. "Come on." He tucked her phone into her left hand and held a hand out to her. "Let me help you over to the fire."

Kaylee glanced in that direction. The three people that remained around the barrel paid no attention to them, instead they all stared at the flames, swaying back and forth.

"They're okay." The man jerked his head toward the others. "They won't hurt you."

The screen on her phone was shattered. She tried pushing the home button anyway, hoping it would still work. No such luck. The spider-webbed screen remained dark. She'd have to trust him. He did just save her from that other man. And he *seemed* sane enough. There was no way she could get to her car in this state, much less drive it.

She raised her hand to his and his fingers closed over hers. He said, "Take it easy. Just stand up real slow. I got ya."

She'd assumed he'd be frail, living on the streets and all, but when she wavered and leaned heavily into his side, he encircled her waist with a strong arm, supporting her weight until she got her balance. Maybe he was newly homeless.

As they neared the fire, one of the three standing around it—a waif of a girl wearing layers of mismatched winter clothing—looked at her with half-lidded eyes. "She okay?"

"She will be. Has a cut head and probably a concussion."

"Good thing Doc Blayne is here to help her out," said a kid that couldn't have been older than thirteen or fourteen. Around the same age as Kaylee's little brother.

"Shut up, dork," Blayne said with a teasing lilt to his voice. "Grab my bag and drag it over here to give her something to lean against."

The boy rolled his eyes but shuffled over to a large duffel bag leaning against a concrete pillar. He dragged it over next to Blayne and Kaylee, then tromped back to his spot by the fire.

"Sit down, lean your back against my bag," Blayne said as he helped her down to the ground. He unzipped his coat and shrugged out of it, then draped it over Kaylee's legs.

"No," Kaylee protested. "It's freezing out here. You'll freeze."

"I'll be fine. Can I take a look at your head, now?"

She nodded and leaned forward.

"It looks like it finally quit bleeding. You should go see your doctor, though. I bet it needs stitches."

Another wave of nausea struck. Kaylee leaned forward, pulling her knees up so she could prop her arms there and rest her forehead on them. The gravel crunched, announcing a new arrival. Kaylee's heart jumped. Had her attacker come back? She lifted her head to see an older woman—barely old enough to be called elderly—walking toward the group, arms loaded with grocery bags.

"Mama C!" the young boy yelled. "It's about time you got back."

The woman stopped in front of Kaylee as Blayne and the others relieved her of the bags. Kaylee greeted the newcomer with a grand mixture of street tacos and bile as she lost her battle with the nausea.

CHAPTER 2

"Here," Mama C held a well-used water bottle out to Kaylee, "take a couple of sips of this. Don't overdo it."

Kaylee tried not to show disgust on her face, but the prospect of drinking out of that bottle made her already-sick stomach turn with greater vigor. She shook her head. "Thank you, but I'm okay."

Mama C looked down at the bottle in her hand, then back at Kaylee. Her face softened in understanding and she handed the water to Blayne. "I'm afraid I don't have any fresh water. That's a luxury we can't often afford here." She smiled, her cracked lips parting to show surprisingly healthy teeth. She raised an eyebrow. "So, what in the world are you doing out here, young lady?"

Heat rushed to her face and Kaylee looked down at her hands. "I...I was looking for you," she whispered.

"You were?" The older woman bent down closer to Kaylee. "Did you say you were looking for me?"

Kaylee nodded.

Squinting, Mama C stared at her until she looked up at her. "Do I know you?"

"No." Kaylee sighed. This was not how she'd wanted this introduction to go. "I'm a college student at CU Denver. I heard about you, about what you're doing here."—she gestured to the teenagers, the grocery bags—"I was...I *am* hoping to interview you as part of a...a school project."

"Hmmf." Mama C frowned and walked away, returning to Kaylee's side a moment later with an upside-down five-gallon bucket on which she sat, muttering, "I can't sit on the ground like you young people. It isn't exactly the sitting that's hard, it's the getting back up part."

"Why do you want to interview her? What kind of 'project' are you doing?" Blayne scowled.

Kaylee swallowed and glanced back and forth between them. "I'm a student."

"Yeah, you already said that," Blayne said.

"Be nice, Blayne," Mama C said. "I'm sure she means no harm."

Kaylee fixed her gaze on the woman. "I want to interview you and maybe observe you for a while. For my master's thesis." Did these people even know what that was?

"I see." Mama C leaned in closer. "What is your major?"

"Psychology."

"And, what is the title of your thesis?"

Mama C, at least, appeared to know what a thesis was. "The working title is, Benevolence and Family-like Groups Among the Homeless." She didn't add the rest of the title—What Drives Even the Hopeless to Desire Family-like Relationships—afraid it would sound insulting to them. She might have to reword that a little.

The woman's mouth tightened for the briefest of moments before relaxing into a neutral expression. "And you thought it would be a good idea to come down to this part of town by yourself, after dark no less?"

"Probably not my brightest idea, huh?" Kaylee shrugged. "This was only supposed to be a reconnaissance mission tonight—I was only planning on observing from a distance. I wasn't even sure this was where you'd be. I've already scoped out several other... umm...areas."

"Ha! Def not a bright idea." The young boy stood by the fire eating a sandwich made hastily from the contents of one of the grocery bags. "I thought college students were supposed to be smart."

Kaylee laid her pounding head back down on her folded arms, ignoring the barb.

"You okay?" Blayne asked.

"My head hurts," she answered. And this wasn't going the way she'd planned. She just wanted to get back to her apartment, take a shower, and go to bed.

"I bet it does," he replied.

"Well," Mama C said. "It's late. And cold. I'm ready to nestle down into my sleeping bag for the night. You'll have to come back around at a more decent time if you want to poke at my brain."

That sounded like a cue to leave. She'd overstayed her dubious welcome. Kaylee lifted her head. "Yes, of course. Will you still be here over the next couple of days?"

"Maybe. Maybe not. We've been here a while. It's probably about time for some other group to come run us off." She frowned, looking from Kaylee to Blayne and back again. "Especially after your little tussle tonight."

Blayne shrugged, purposefully, it seemed, avoiding Kaylee's gaze. "I couldn't just let that guy hurt her."

Mama C stood, wincing at the effort, and patted his arm. "I know you couldn't. And I wouldn't have expected you to." She looked down at Kaylee. "How did you get here, dear?"

"I drove. My car is parked about a half-block away."

Blayne raised his eyebrows. "Hopefully it's still in one piece." He reached a hand toward her. "Let's see if you're well enough to drive."

Grasping his hand, she stood slowly, careful not to let his coat drop to the ground. A slight feeling of dizziness threatened, but not nearly as bad as before. She straightened up, removed her hand from his, and handed him his coat. "I'm okay. Much better. Thank you." She patted her pockets, relieved to find that her keys were still tucked safely away in her jacket.

"I'll walk you to your car." Not waiting for an answer, he started walking in the direction of where she'd been attacked.

"You really don't have to." The tiny quaver in her voice gave her away. Fear tore at her insides at the thought of walking the short distance alone.

He slowed when he reached the area she'd been observing from. "Where's your car from here?"

Kaylee pointed past two overflowing dumpsters where a small section of her rear bumper could be seen.

Shaking his head, Blayne muttered, "That's the worst possible place you could have parked, college girl."

Normally, that kind of assumption of her naivety would have riled her—and it kind of still did—but she just wanted to get to her car and get home where she could take a shower and go to bed.

"Did you at least have the sense to lock the doors?" He stopped and faced her a few yards from the dumpsters.

A tired sigh pushed through her pursed lips and she put a hand on her hip. "Of course, I did." She pulled her keys out of her jacket pocket and put her thumb on the unlock button of the fob.

"Not yet." Blayne put his hand over hers to stop her from pushing it. "Let me make sure no one's lurking around."

He jogged to the back of her car and around to the far side where she could no longer see him. A moment later he reappeared around the other side of the dumpsters.

Kaylee raised an eyebrow at him as he approached.

"All clear," he said. "It looks like your car is intact, too. You got lucky."

She could hear the condescension in his voice—and this time she couldn't ignore it. "I'm not stupid, you know. I know this area is dangerous. I was only planning to stay for a few minutes."

He looked down. "I never said you were stupid. But you do seem a little unaware of the danger around here." He glanced back up. "Anyway, you should be going." He turned and walked around to the driver's side of her car and stood, waiting for her to catch up.

With a roll of her eyes, she joined him and pushed the unlock button. She reached for the door handle and her hand collided with his. Pulling away, she let him open the door for her. She looked into his eyes as he gestured for her to get in. He was definitely not what she expected from a homeless man. His eyes were clear and intense.

He was able-bodied as far as she could tell. Why was he here? A rush of heat flowed to her cheeks as she realized she'd been staring at him for much longer than necessity would dictate under the circumstances. She cleared her throat and averted her gaze. "Thank you. Have a good night." *That was a dumb thing to say*, she thought as she hurriedly slid into her seat and slammed the door.

She started her car and risked one more glance at this strange young rescuer. His eyebrows were drawn into a scowl, but she could swear his lips twitched into the hint of a smile just before she backed up then sped away toward the freeway. She would have to try to get his story. Hopefully Mama C and her group would still be there when she came back.

The clock on her dashboard read 1:25. Holy crap! She'd been there for a couple of hours. Touching the sticky mess at the back of her head, she groaned and remembered Blayne saying she'd need some stitches. She weighed the consequences of just going back to her apartment and dealing with the cut the next day or going to the ER to get it taken care of tonight. She thought about the filthy ground she'd bounced her head off of and her mind instantly turned to what possible substances could be found there. "Ugh. ER it is," she said. "I probably need a tetanus shot, anyway."

IT WAS after four in the morning when Kaylee trudged up the stairs to the second-floor apartment she shared with Allie, the first friend she'd made Freshman year. Her greatest desire at that moment was to go flop into bed and sleep for about twelve hours straight, but the cute doctor that stitched her up had repeated several times that she needed to take a shower immediately when she got home. And then keep her wound mostly dry for the next seven days until she had the sutures removed. Thankfully she didn't have to work as a TA or go to class that morning.

After the shower, she stood in front of the small circle she'd wiped clear on the steam-covered mirror, brush in hand. She'd detangled most of her hair—all but the area around the goose-egg and sutures. She gently put the brush to the matted tangles and winced as soon as it tugged. "Gah!" She threw the brush onto the countertop. "Not happening today. Maybe I'll just get my hair all chopped off," she whispered.

She opened the door to her bedroom. She slipped inside and felt her way to the raised twin bed on her side of the shared room, hoping Allie was sound asleep. Kaylee fumbled with the mess of sheets and blankets piled on her mattress. Maybe she should start making her bed once in a while. She crawled onto the bed, laying on her side so as not to put pressure on her aching head, and pulled a corner of her blanket over her.

Mission accomplished, no movement from Allie's side of the room. Kaylee sighed and closed her eyes.

"Don't think we aren't going to talk about where you've been," Allie mumbled. "It can wait till sometime after the sun comes up, though." Covers ruffled as she turned over.

Why did she have to get stuck with a light-sleeper as a roommate and best friend? The fact that she was deaf didn't seem to make her any heavier of a sleeper. Kaylee swore she could feel the vibrations in the room like a spider can feel its web jerking when prey flies into it. She smiled and kicked her blankets into a better position. It wasn't like she didn't plan on telling Allie everything, anyway.

CHAPTER 3

"So, let me get this straight." Allie stopped tugging at the knots in Kaylee's hair so she could step in front of her and glare into her bloodshot eyes. "You went down there, at night, all by yourself?"

"Well, yeah, but I was just *observing*. I didn't think..." *Maybe if I mumble she won't be able to read my lips*, Kaylee thought with a grimace.

"Exactly. You didn't think." Allie put a hand on her hip and pointed the hairbrush at Kaylee's face. "Do you think your professors would approve of your dangerous methods?"

"Maybe they'll give me extra credit for going above and beyond." Her friend didn't smile at her attempt to lighten the mood.

"And, if I'd known that you had a head injury, I wouldn't have let you sleep so long. Why didn't you tell me about this when you first got home?"

Kaylee shrugged. "I didn't want to wake you up or keep you awake. I know how much you hate early mornings. Plus, I just wanted to sleep." Although, as exhausted as she'd been, it had taken her at least an hour to fall asleep, her brain refusing to let go of the evening's events.

"Well, hopefully you learned your lesson. No more traipsing around downtown by yourself." She moved back behind Kaylee to continue with the painful process of untangling her hair. "Maybe you should consider changing your thesis to something a little less life-threatening."

"Are you crazy?" Kaylee's eyes met her friend's in the mirror. "I finally found her! There's no way I'm backing out of this now."

"You have no way of knowing where she'll be when we get back from Christmas break. You'll have to start the hunt all over again." She laid the brush on the kitchen table next to the propped-up mirror. "I got most of them. You'll just have to get to the rest after the stitches are out."

Christmas break. That would be a problem. Finals started on Monday, tomorrow, and then school would be out for weeks. Her parents expected her to come home during those weeks between semesters. "Thanks." Kaylee absently ran her hand down the hair at the back of her head. "Maybe I'll just stay here for the break."

"Oh, your parents would love that." Allie's voice overflowed with sarcasm.

"No, I'm serious." Kaylee leaned toward her friend. "You and Max will be here most of that time, right? Because Max has rotations he has to complete?"

Allie narrowed her eyes and answered with a drawn out, "Yeah. Why?"

"You'll be able to keep an eye on me." Kaylee smiled. "Make sure I don't do something else stupid."

She rolled her eyes. "Sheesh. Do you remember when *I* was the one who needed to be babysat?" Her sophomore year had been a rough one. Too many alcohol-fueled frat parties. Kaylee hadn't dared let her out of her sight.

Kaylee nodded. "I'm so glad you grew out of that rebellious stage."

"I blame Max. He's such a good influence." She slumped into a chair and looked down at the table. "Seriously, I wouldn't be graduating from nursing school in May if it wasn't for him, and for you."

Kaylee patted her friend's hand, waiting for her to look up. "You would have pulled out of it, eventually. Now, how do I tell my parents I won't be coming home for Christmas?"

Allie raised an eyebrow. "You're serious about this, aren't you?"

Nodding, Kaylee answered, "I am. After meeting Mama C last

night, I think I'd want to find out more about her even if my thesis didn't depend on it. There's something very different with her and her little gang."

HER PARENTS HAD TAKEN the news about as well as she'd expected. Kaylee stared at the follow-up text her mom had sent after the tearful phone call.

I'm sorry I got upset. You do what you need to do for school. We'll see you over spring break. I'm so proud of you. Love you. ~Mom

Kaylee smiled at the last part. No matter how many times she told her mom she didn't need to sign her texts, she still did. Just like the little notes she used to leave her. She typed out a quick response before heading off to take her first final.

It's okay. Spring break for sure. Love you too.

The crumbs from her toast would have to wait until she got back to be cleaned up. She shoved the last piece in her mouth and wiped her hands on her jeans before grabbing her coat and backpack.

Her test didn't go as well as it should have. She had a hard time concentrating. The ER doctor had told her that might happen because of the concussion. But besides being a little foggy, her mind kept wandering to Mama C. And Blayne. And the others whose names she didn't know or couldn't remember.

She signed off the computer at the testing center, gathered her belongings from the bored-looking proctor there to keep students from cheating, and started the long trek back to her car. *I should go home and finish grading the Psych 1100 papers.* She looked up at the clear sky, the sun just past its peak. It would be hours before it started to get dark. *My thesis is more important than getting those papers back quickly. I should go talk to Mama C while she's still where I can find her. Hopefully.*

She'd made up her mind before she reached her car. There would be plenty of time to grade papers later, and there was no telling how long Mama C's group would be at the viaduct. She'd hate to have to start her search all over again.

This time Kaylee parked where she'd still be able to see her car from the fire barrel. She walked with caution toward those gathered there, searching for the familiar faces from Saturday night. Heart pounding in her throat, she stopped and stared down at the bloodstained gravel. She glanced over her shoulder, paranoia gripping her chest as she half expected her attacker to be there, leering at her. She released the breath she'd been holding when she saw that no one lurked there.

Turning back to the ragtag group, she caught Blayne's eye for a split second before he looked back down to continue his task of shoving things into his well-worn backpack. "You came back," he called, without looking up.

"Yep."

"How's your head?"

She touched the still tender but healing cut held together with seven stitches. "Getting better." She stopped several paces in front of him and looked around. "There are a lot less people here than there was the other night. Where is everyone?"

"Oh, you know, out goofing off. It's a carefree life we homeless live." He looked up at her, one eye nearly closed in a scowl. "What you really want to know is where Mama C is."

"I want to know that *too*." She had no idea how to respond to his obvious annoyance with her. "I just...are you...am I bugging you?"

The zipper on his pack stuck as he tried to close it. He yanked on it then cussed when it broke off in his hand. "Yeah, you kind of are." He sighed and stood to face her. "Look, I don't know what you think you're going to get out of her, what you think you'll gain by digging into her business then going back to your cozy little dorm room or whatever. Back to your safe little world where daddy's credit card takes care of your every need. But Mama's doing good things here, and she doesn't talk about her past or why she's homeless. It takes her to a dark place. And these kids need her to not be in that dark place."

"What about you? Do you need her?" Kaylee decided to ignore his jab about her daddy's credit card. If he only knew how hard she'd worked to get and keep scholarships so her lower-middle class parents didn't have to worry about supporting her.

He slung his backpack across his right shoulder. "No. Not like I used to."

"Then why are you still with her?"

"To protect her." He stared down at Kaylee, the piercing blue of his eyes nearly knocking her to the ground. "And because she's home to me."

"Home?" Kaylee caught up and walked alongside him as he stepped away.

"Yeah. Home isn't always a place. Sometimes it's a person."

They walked in silence, Kaylee glancing behind her as the distance from her car increased.

Blayne stopped and looked down at her. "You aren't going to let this go, are you?"

She shook her head, mesmerized again by the clear blue eyes peeking out from behind his straggly hair.

"Fine. Then I have some rules for you. One rule, actually. Don't push her to tell you about her past."

"Okay." She nodded to reaffirm her sincerity. "Okay. I won't."

He stared at her for a few seconds then continued walking.

"Wait." Kaylee looked back at her car again. "Where are you going?"

He turned and walked backward, raising an eyebrow. "Why do you want to know?"

"Can I buy you lunch?" she blurted out, warmth flooding her cheeks as she clamped her mouth shut on the words she hadn't meant to utter.

"Lunch?"

"Um, yeah. I...I'd like to ask you some more questions."

"For your *thesis*? I thought you needed Mama C for that?"

"She's the main focus, but the paper will involve your whole group." She jerked her head back toward her car. "Come on. We can go wherever you want—on a poor college student's budget."

Blayne licked his lips. "Aren't you scared to be alone with me?"

"Should I be?" She probably should be. Why wasn't she? Was it because he'd saved her a couple of nights ago? Was it the tender protectiveness he showed for Mama C? Was it the ocean-blue of his eyes?

"Yeah. Not because I'm planning to hurt you, but because you don't *know* that I'm not going to hurt you. You don't know *me*."

"I'll take that chance." What was she thinking? "Where do you want to eat?"

He looked down at his dirty, worn clothes. "I'm not exactly dressed for a restaurant."

Kaylee bit her lip, thinking. "We can do pick-up and eat in the car where it's warm."

He stepped toward her and pulled on his beard. "I haven't showered in, like, a while. You sure you want that stench in your car?"

"I have an air freshener." She grinned and shrugged. "Come on. Where do you want to go?"

WATCHING the endless line of cars parading down the busy street in front of her, Kaylee reached for another fry. "So, you haven't eaten at a restaurant for who knows how long, and you choose McDonald's?"

"They have the best fries."

She couldn't argue with that logic.

He chewed then swallowed a large bite of his hamburger. "Go ahead and ask me."

"Ask you what?" She'd been stalling. She had so many questions for him but was afraid of insulting or annoying him. She really didn't want to rekindle the anger she'd seen from him earlier.

"You know. 'Why are you homeless?' 'You look normal, why don't you have a job?' 'Does your family know where you are?'" He took a long draw of his drink. "That's what this lunch was all about, wasn't it? Because you want to ask me some questions?"

Yep. Those were the questions that had been racing through her mind. "Why don't you just tell me whatever you're comfortable with, and I'll ask some follow-up questions. And you can answer the ones you want and ignore the ones you don't want to answer."

"Okay." He wiped ketchup off his beard with a napkin. "Don't you need to take notes or something?"

She peeked in the back seat. She hadn't brought her backpack with her. "I have a pretty good memory—as long as I write everything down as soon as I get home."

His eyes bore into hers for several seconds before he turned away to stare out through the windshield. She released the breath she hadn't realized she'd been holding. His eyes. So clear. So deep. She could sense strength and intelligence in their depths—not at all what she expected to see in the eyes of someone living on the streets.

"I'm homeless," he started, "because I left home before my parents had to make the choice to kick me out a few years ago." He turned his head to look out the side window. "They should have made me leave so much sooner." His haunting voice grew quiet.

"How old were you?"

"Nineteen."

That made him just slightly younger than her. "Why?" she whispered.

"Drugs. I was a druggie." He turned back to her, searching her eyes as if trying to decide how much to tell her. How far to go. He closed his eyes and blew out a breath. "I put my little sister in danger —I could see that even through the haze of the drugs."

Again, Kaylee thought about how clear his eyes looked, how coherent he spoke, how strong he'd felt when he'd helped her to stand in her semi-conscious state the other night. None of those things fit with what she knew about drug addicts. "You said you *were* a druggie, past tense."

He popped another fry in his mouth and waited until he'd chewed and swallowed it to answer. "I didn't mean to misrepresent myself, here. Once an addict, always an addict. But I have been sober for about six months."

Each of his answers brought more questions to her mind. "That's great. I mean, that's *really* great. How..."

"How did I stop?"

Kaylee nodded.

"I met Mama C." He smiled. "Her number one rule is that if you want to stay in her gang, you have one month to get clean and stay clean. She doesn't tolerate any slip-ups."

This was the trail she needed to follow for her thesis. She forced the other questions down and asked, "What drew you to her? What does she do for you and the others that would persuade you to stop? I mean, if you wouldn't stop for your family, why for her?"

"I don't know." His chin rested on his chest as he stared down at his hands. "I wasn't ready before. The drugs had such a hold on me, all I could think about was where I was going to get my next fix." He paused, lifting a finger to his mouth to chew on his nail. "I was near starved to death when Mama C came across me in an alley. I have no idea how long it'd been since I'd last eaten anything. Days. Weeks, maybe. I hadn't shot up in a couple of days and the withdrawal was horrible. I honestly just wanted to curl up in that alley and die like the worthless piece of shit I am."

"No." She reached for his arm.

He flinched away from her touch. "Mama wouldn't let me. She brought me food. A sleeping bag. A coat. She sat with me and nursed me back to health."

"Why does she do it?"

Clearing his throat, he sat up straighter. "You'll have to ask her that."

His tone of voice suggested that his cooperation with her questions was coming to an end. She tried for one more. "Now that you're clean—why don't you go home?"

He barked out a short, humorless laugh. "Thanks for lunch. I need to get going now." He opened the car door and ducked to get out.

"Wait. I can take you back."

"Nah. Thanks, but I feel like walking."

"When will Mama C be back?"

"She doesn't keep a regular schedule, college girl. You'll just have to keep checking back." He slammed the door and shouldered his backpack as he strode off.

Kaylee slumped down, pressing her back into the seat. One of the first rules of psychology was to not get emotionally involved with your patients, or, in this instance, with the subjects of your research. Stay detached. Always look at things from the outside. With the first interview, she'd already broken that rule. She closed her eyes and tried to breathe through the tightening of her chest.

CHAPTER 4

Kaylee slowed her car and pulled off to the side of the road, creeping up just enough to see past the curve behind her yet still staying out of sight of the group laughing around the fire. She wanted to talk to Mama C alone—without her gang of protective followers nearby.

Twisting in her seat, she glanced at the door lock to ensure it was in the down position even though she'd checked it multiple times already. She let her gaze fall to the street and sidewalk behind her. That had been the direction Mama C had come from last time. Kaylee drummed her fingers on the steering wheel. She tried to convince herself she was safe inside the car, but she knew she wasn't. Nothing a good crowbar couldn't fix for someone truly intent on getting to her. "I won't stay past dark," she said out loud.

A kink in her neck forced her to turn back to the front. She glanced at the clock in her dash and her heart sank. It would be dark within forty minutes. She adjusted the rearview mirror and watched the street through it.

Kaylee growled as the sky darkened. She sighed and took one last look behind her. "Oh, well. I really need to study for that test tomorrow, anyway." She started the car but didn't turn the headlights on. She eased into the road and turned around, not wanting Mama's gang to see her. Not wanting Blayne to know she'd been there.

She turned onto a main street and clicked her headlights on.

"How'd I do?"

Kaylee smiled at the guy who'd sat on the front row all semester but had only uttered a few words that whole time. "How do you think you did?" She'd just finished proctoring the Psych 1100 final for the professor she TA'd for.

His face flushed, and he shrugged. "Art History is my major. I'm not that into Psych."

Kaylee zipped up her jacket and shoved her pencil into her bag before throwing one strap over her right shoulder. "See ya' later."

The quiet guy caught up to her in two steps. "Wait."

She hesitated, frowning before she turned to face him.

He must have caught the tail-end of the frown in her eyes because he dropped his gaze to his hands and cleared his throat. "I...I was just wondering if you'd like to go get lunch. With me."

"Um, I'm seeing someone. I'm sorry." Why had she said that? She hadn't been on a date in months. And Shy-Guy was kinda cute.

"Oh. Sorry."

"It's okay, it's a new thing. I just don't want to mess it up before we see where it's going." More lies. What was she doing?

"I...I understand." He started walking beside her. "What's his name?" Did his voice hold a hint of disbelief? Or was that her guilt tricking her ears into hearing it that way?

"Blayne," she spat out. She slapped a hand to her mouth and tried to cover the reaction with a lame cough. *Blayne? Really? The homeless guy?* She rolled her eyes. *Way to set your standards high.*

"Is he a student here?"

"No. No. He isn't a student. He works with the homeless." She needed to get away from her prying classmate before her nose started growing. "I'm meeting him for lunch downtown. And then I have papers to grade for the professor. Sorry again. Gotta go." She sped up to a near jog and didn't turn back to see if he'd followed her.

She'd parked her car on the street; money was too tight to pay for a parking permit on campus. She slowed to a normal pace after a couple of minutes, sure she'd left him in her wake.

The walk to her car seemed to take hours. She threw her backpack in the passenger seat and slammed the driver's side door. Drumming her fingers on the steering wheel, she thought, *What am I going to do now?* Her plan had been to grab a bite to eat from the cafeteria then spend the rest of the time studying before her last final in two hours. She'd have to drive somewhere to get lunch and just study there.

Even though she drove herself there, she looked up in shock to see she'd ended up, not at a fast-food joint as she'd planned, but at the viaduct. She slowly shifted the car into park and stared at the lone figure beneath the bridge as she turned off the engine. "Mama C," she whispered. With no one else around to interfere.

The older woman looked up sharply as Kaylee shut the car door. Kaylee didn't take her eyes off the woman who didn't exactly smile, but didn't scowl either. That was good, right?

Kaylee smiled as she approached.

Mama C put a hand on her hip, pursed her lips, then said, "Hmm. I kinda' thought you'd give up after your last visit. How's your head?"

Biting her lip, Kaylee ran her fingers down the sutures she'd need to get taken out soon. "It's fine. Nothing a few stitches couldn't fix." She took another step closer. "Do you have time to talk right now?"

Mama C snorted out a laugh. "I suppose I could spare a little time out of my busy schedule." She gestured to a couple of upside-down buckets. "Have a seat."

Kaylee, glad she'd worn an older pair of jeans, brushed some ashes off the top of a bucket and sat down, zipping her coat further up her neck to help fight off the chill air.

"Well," Mama C grunted as she lowered herself onto a bucket. "What questions ya' got for me? And just so you know, I'm not gonna tell you my whole life's story. Nobody gets to know that but me."

Kaylee frowned, looking down to get a notebook and pen out of her backpack. "Fair enough. Let's start with your name, maybe? Everyone calls you 'Mama C'—what's your real name?"

With a shake of her head and a waggling of her finger, she answered, "Nope. That's one of those things you don't get to know."

"Not even your first name?"

Mama C pulled her eyebrows together.

"Please?" Kaylee begged.

"Fine. Guess it won't hurt to tell you that." She looked Kaylee straight in the eyes. "My name's Claire."

"Great," Kaylee said with a smile. "What..."

"You can call me Mama C, just like everyone else. Don't go around spreadin' my name around like it's your business."

"Of course." Was this woman really the benevolent angel others had claimed her to be? She seemed kind of ornery. Like Kaylee's Aunt Helen. She'd have to steer clear of questions about her past—for now. "Can you tell me about the group of young people you...uh...you live with here on the streets?"

"They're just some young people I try to help. And they help me."

"How do you find them? Or do they find you?"

"Both. I find some, and some look for me because they hear I might have food."

"Do you accept anyone into your group? Or do you have rules?" Kaylee already knew there were some stipulations, Blayne had told her that.

"No drugs, no fighting, everyone helps if there's work to be done."

"And, you feed them. I saw that you brought them food. What else do you do? What else is it that brings these street-kids to you?"

Mama C sighed and looked down at her filthy gloved hands. "It's like you said when you told me the name of your thesis. Some people just crave a family-like environment. Some of these kids ran from some horrible pasts and some of them made their own horrible present and ran because of that. So, we become the new family together. And I'm the matriarch. I feed them and make sure they're warm. They take care of me in other ways."

"Why?" Kaylee whispered. "Why do you do this?"

Kaylee had to lean in to hear the response, spoken so quietly. "A mother's instinct never goes away."

Kaylee forgot the next several questions she'd planned to ask and blurted out, "You have kids? Or *had* kids?"

Grunting as she stood, Mama C wiped a single tear from her face. "Interview over. I've got things to do." She stepped away and turned to glare at Kaylee still glued to her spot. With a shooing motion, she growled, "Off with you now." Her face softened a touch when she looked into Kaylee's eyes. "I'll meet you at Brews and Things tonight at four o'clock if you want—but no more questions about my personal life." She pointed at Kaylee with a stern finger and turned and walked away.

CHAPTER 5

Kaylee slipped inside just before the professor shut the door. She'd nearly forgotten about her last final and she certainly hadn't done any extra studying like she'd planned.

The first question on the test stared back at her from the white page. In the background she faintly perceived the scratching of pencils on paper. Her own pencil remained still in her hand, the words on the paper blurring as she replayed her short conversation with Mama C over again in her mind.

"Kaylee!!"

The hushed whisper caused her to jump and almost drop her pencil. She stole a quick glance at her friend, Jamie, sitting next to her. Jamie gestured at her own test then went right back to furiously scribbling down answers. Kaylee's eyes widened as she looked up at the clock. Ten minutes had ticked by and she hadn't even read the first question of this thirty-minute timed test!

Pushing thoughts of her thesis aside, she rushed through the test in the remaining twenty-minutes.

KAYLEE PARKED in front of the coffee shop and drew in a steadying breath. She'd written down the questions she would ask, not necessarily the ones she *wanted* to ask, though. A hard rap on her window. She jumped in her seat, and her heart vaulted into her throat. She scowled and looked to her left. Blayne stood there, laughing at her, Mama C by his side. Kaylee wiped the scowl from her face and opened the door to hear Mama C chastising him. "You shouldn't go around scaring people like that. Shame on you. Look, her face is all red, now."

"That's just...uh...I must have had my heater on too high." Kaylee looked at the ground as the heat in her face burned hotter.

"Sorry, Kaylee." He still had a hint of mischief in his voice. "Let's go inside where it's warm."

He opened the door for them and Kaylee leaned into Mama C and said, "I didn't know he was coming."

Shaking her head, the older woman replied, "He insisted. Says he wants to make sure I'm protected, but I'm not so sure that's the reason he's taggin' along."

"Why..." Kaylee didn't get to finish her question.

"There's a table right over there," Blayne caught up to them. "You buyin' Kaylee?"

"Umm, yes, of course." Thinking about her abysmal bank account, she hoped they just wanted coffee.

"Just kidding, we can get our own." Blayne stood behind her in line. "What, do you think we're homeless or something?"

She turned to look at him, her mouth slightly open, and he winked at her. She shut her mouth and narrowed her eyes a little. "I'd like to buy your drinks, if that's okay, since Mama C is helping me with my thesis."

He shrugged. "If that's what you want."

"It is. Why don't you tell me what you want so you two can go save that table for us? I'll bring our order over there."

"Coffee. Black."

"Same here," said Mama C. "None of that fancy fru-fru stuff for me."

Kaylee carried their two black coffees and her "fru-fru" vanilla cappuccino over to the table, sat next to Mama C, and pulled her notebook and pen out. "So, Blayne. I hear you're afraid I might be a danger to Mama C?" Despite her proclivity to flush with embarrassment at the slightest thing, she wanted to show him she could be strong and confront people if she felt the need.

"Huh," he looked at Mama C, "did you tell her that?"

"I tell it like I see it." Mama C sipped at her coffee.

Blayne shook his head and quirked his mouth into a half smile. "I don't see you as a physical danger, obviously. But you might be an emotional—or just annoying—danger to her. So, I'm just here to make sure that doesn't happen."

"I would never," Kaylee started to deny that she was any such danger, but then remembered how their earlier conversation had ended. She cleared her throat. "I would never *intentionally* hurt her in any way."

"And," Mama C interrupted. "I'm sitting right here, you two young hooligans. And, if I feel she's gettin' too personal, I'll just get up and walk away. Isn't that right, young lady?"

Kaylee nodded and looked at Blayne. "But you're welcome to stay anyway so I can prove to you how innocuous I am."

He rolled his eyes. "Do all you college girls use big words?"

"Oh, I'm sorry. Innocuous means..."

He leaned over the table, closer to her. "I know what it means."

She squirmed in her chair and took a big sip of her still-steaming cappuccino. "Ow! Hot!" It burned all the way down until it splashed into her stomach.

The smirk on Blayne's face turned to one of concern as the corners of his mouth wilted into a frown. "I'll go get you some ice." He pushed his chair back into the person sitting behind him and hurried to the counter to ask for a cup of ice.

"See," Mama C said. "My Blayne isn't so bad."

Kaylee smiled despite her burning tongue and throat and watering eyes.

"Here." Blayne slammed the cup of ice onto the table in front of her. "I've done that before. It burns all the way down. You should have spit it out."

She crunched a piece of ice and let the coolness slide down her throat. "Don't think I didn't consider doing just that. I didn't want to spray it all over you, though."

He laughed for real this time. A beautiful, short laugh. "You're my hero. Thanks for not spewing your fru-fru drink all over me. I'd hate to have to take this," he gestured to his battered, dirty, worn coat, "to the dry-cleaners again so soon."

"You're welcome." Kaylee smiled but didn't quite dare to laugh at his self-deprecating joke.

"Let's get started, shall we," Mama C said. "I'd like to get back home before it gets too dark."

Kaylee drew in a breath and sat the cup down. "Okay. We talked a little this morning about some of the kids, or young people, you help. Can you tell me more about them? About their backgrounds?" She glanced at Blayne then back at Mama C and quickly added, "Not names and stuff, just some general information."

"You know theirs aren't my stories to tell. You'll have to come back to the viaduct with us and ask them yourself if you want to know their tales."

Tapping her pen on the table, Kaylee tried not to show her frustration, even though she'd been sure that would be the woman's answer. She nodded. "Okay, I'll do that. How about just some general numbers? How long have you been homeless?"

"Right around ten years, I suppose." Her eyes faded out of focus for a moment.

"About how many young people have you helped over the years?" asked Kaylee.

"Hmm. Now that's a harder number to come by."

While Mama C sipped her coffee and thought, Kaylee looked around the coffee shop. Two police officers in the corner stared at them and whispered. One caught her eye and frowned, mouthing "you okay" as he pointed at her. She nodded and smiled to show she was in no distress.

"What was that all about? Flirting with our fine men in blue, are you?" asked Blayne.

"No, no. I...he..."

"Oh, wait." Blayne scowled. "I think I know what happened. He saw you here with us and was just making sure you're okay. That we aren't forcing you to be in our presence. Is that it?"

"There isn't one thing wrong with that, Blayne," Mama C said. "You know we look like a couple of deranged druggies in our old clothes and unbathed states. Now quit glaring at those nice policemen. Kaylee and I have things to discuss.

"Now, what was it you asked me?"

Kaylee looked at her notebook and answered, "How many young people have you helped over the years?"

"That's right. I really don't know. Could be fifty, could be a hundred. I don't keep track. If they need help and are willing to live with my rules, they're welcome." She slapped her hand on the table in front of Blayne. "Stop giving the evil eye to those police."

Blayne turned his gaze on Mama and softened it as he took in a breath. "I'm going to go get a refill, do you want one Mama C?"

"No, thank you."

As Blayne made his way to the counter, Kaylee asked, "Can you tell me about any of your past kids? Not specifics, just in general? Why they became homeless maybe and if...if there were any happy endings?" Her eyes flicked to Blayne, his hand tapped his thigh in rhythm to the music playing over the store speakers.

"Oh, there are always happy endings, dear." She patted Kaylee's hand. "Sometimes..." her eyes glazed over again, "sometimes even death can be a happy ending." She shook her head and focused on Kaylee. "The ones that do well are those who clean up their act and go back to their families. Unfortunately, not everyone has a family they can go back to."

Was she referring to herself? Kaylee wondered.

Blayne sat back down with his refill. He shook his head. "I really miss my stereo." He looked at Mama C. "We should be going soon. This place is getting crowded and I hate being stared at by these people who, you know, have a life."

"Come on now, Blayne," Mama C said. "You have a life, too. Just not as *clean* or *warm* as theirs." She turned to Kaylee. "Do you want to come back with us and talk to the kids? There are at least two who I'm sure will share their stories with you—they share them with everyone else often enough." She shook her head.

Kaylee perked up. "Yes. Thank you. I'd love to go talk to them."

On their way back to the viaduct, Kaylee quizzed Blayne about what kind of music he liked, surprised to find they had similar tastes.

CHAPTER 6

The sun dipped behind the horizon as they pulled up to the viaduct. Kaylee readjusted the scarf around her neck as she stepped out into the bitter cold, wondering how anyone could survive the cold winters of Denver with nowhere to sleep but the streets. The slanted sides of the viaduct only helped slightly to tame the wind. The orange glow from the fire barrel called to her like a Phoenix song. *This is their lifeline*, she thought, as the three people surrounding it made room for her, Blayne, and Mama C.

She fought back tears, wishing she could bring them all back to her tiny, warm apartment. Her thoughts were interrupted by Mama C.

"You all remember Kaylee." She looked around at the small group of young people. "She'd like to hear some of your stories, if you're willing to talk."

A black boy who looked to be younger than her little brother, cocked his head to the side and asked, "Why do you want to know our stories?"

Kaylee cleared her throat. "I...I'm writing a thesis about Mama C and I'd like to...uh...to add your stories in. To show how she's helped you and how you got here."

"That's cool." The boy adjusted his beanie. "I'm Demarcus. What do you wanna know?"

With a quick glance at Blayne before looking back at Demarcus, she asked, "How did you become homeless?"

"Well, now, ya' see. My story's a little different from these losers." He slapped a thin blonde girl on the shoulder.

"Demarcus..." Mama C warned.

"Just kidding, just kidding. Don't kill me in my sleep, Blayne." He turned back to Kaylee. "I just mean that it wasn't really things I *did* to get me here, but who I *am* that got me here."

"What do you mean?" Kaylee asked.

"Well, I'm out here 'cuz I'm gay." He focused on the flames from which he warmed his hands. His eyes changed in an instant from the sparkling of a teasing teen, to the dullness of someone with a heart full of hurt. "My dad caught me with the star senior of my high school football team. I was a freshman at the time. The dude grabbed his clothes and ran. I don't really blame him, my dad's a big guy."

The crackling of the fire and the distant hum of cars were the only sounds for several seconds. Afraid to hear the rest, but still wanting to know, Kaylee asked, "What happened then? What did your dad do?"

He looked at her, a flash of anger coloring his eyes. "What do you think he did? He was furious. He yelled at me. Called me names. Said, 'no son of mine is going to be a homo.' And, 'your mother would be so disappointed, I'm glad she isn't here to see this.'"

"Where's your mom?"

"Dead. My mom's dead. She died of cancer when I was six."

"I'm sorry. So, your dad kicked you out?"

Demarcus's eyes flicked back to the fire. "I knew he was gonna. So I just saved him the trouble of saying the words. I packed up and got the hell out of there."

In a quiet voice, Kaylee asked, "How old are you?"

"Fifteen."

"How long have you been out here?"

"Almost a year."

"How did you find Mama C?"

The tightness in his jaws relaxed, and the anger was replaced with tenderness as he looked at the older woman. "She found me. I'd tried to find a job, but no one will hire you—at least for legal stuff—when you're under sixteen. I was starving and desperate. I decided to go in search of one of the illegal jobs a fourteen-year-old could do. I was from the suburbs, man. I didn't know how things worked in the streets. Instead of getting a job, I got myself beat up." He nodded toward Mama C. "Mama here found me at my worst. All bloodied up, clothes ripped to shreds, near starved to death."

Kaylee looked down at her hands to hide the horror she was sure showed on her face. This poor boy. She shook her head and asked one more question. "When was this? When did Mama C find you?"

He shrugged. "Maybe five, six months ago. She gave me clothes and food and brought me back to be part of her little family."

"Tell her about the goals you've set, D." Mama C nodded encouragement.

"Well, Mama wants me to go back to school, but that ain't as easy as it sounds when you have nowhere to live. My goal is to get a job when I turn sixteen. Mama's gonna help me get a state I.D. and some decent clothes to interview in. Until then, Mama's helping me stay up on my studies."

"You do have some other options, since you're underage—" Kaylee started.

"Like what?" Demarcus interrupted. "Foster care? No thanks."

Since foster care was exactly what she'd been thinking, Kaylee decided it was time to move on to someone else. "Okay. Um, does anyone else want to tell me their story?"

"Ha. No way," the thin, blonde girl whispered. "Why would I want to tell you about my shame? So you and your college buddies can judge me?"

"Hannah," Mama C chided. "Kaylee isn't here to judge anyone. And she asked for volunteers, if you don't want to be one then don't. No need to be rude."

Hannah sniffed and wiped her face. She backed away from the fire and sat on a sleeping bag laid out a few feet away. Mama C's eyes followed her, showing only tenderness.

"I'll talk to you. I'm an open book." The older teen brushed his greasy hair out of his face.

Blayne snorted. "Yeah, a book no one wants to read, Clint."

"Yeah, well, it looks like your girlfriend wants to *read my book.*"

Blayne's eyes flicked to Kaylee's face then back at Clint. "Huh, I wouldn't date a college girl. They're too snooty for me."

Like I would date a homeless guy, Kaylee thought, the heat rising to her face. Ignoring the sting his words left deep inside, she avoided looking at him and smiled at Clint instead. "I'd love to hear your story, Clint."

"Hah! Told you, Blayne." Clint laughed. "Mine isn't as dramatic as Demarcus's. I turned eighteen and left home to pursue legal pot. I couldn't wait to move to Colorado, where I could partake to my heart's content and not have to worry about going to jail. I didn't count on the fact that others of my ilk had the same idea. Or that, even in a state where it's legal, no one wants to hire a pothead."

"Yeah," Kaylee said. "I've heard that many employers still do drug testing and won't hire you if it's in your system, even though it is legal here."

"Even after I figured that out, though, I was like, 'no big deal! I'll just get a job at one of the pot shops!'" He shrugged. "Come to find out, they don't really like to hire people who might be tempted to try out their wares. Skim a little off the top. Help themselves."

"How long have you been here, in Colorado?"

"About nine months."

"Why didn't you just go home when you couldn't find a job?"

"No way to get home. Plus, my parents have a rule—once you move out, you aren't allowed to move back in. And I doubt they'd bend that rule for me. I was pretty much a douchebag when I left. They weren't real thrilled about my choice of pot as an antianxiety fix, ya' know?"

She knew. Sort of. Her parents would not have taken that well, either. Just one more question and she'd leave. It had become increasingly uncomfortable since Clint's "girlfriend" remark and Blayne's tart answer. "How did you find Mama C?"

"I heard about her. One of the old bums over by the city hall saw me begging a hotdog stand owner for some food. He told me where to find her and that she might be able to hook me up with something to eat."

"And he's been hanging around ever since," Mama C said. She shuffled over to her upside-down bucket and lowered herself with a grunt. "He's been off the weed for long enough now that he needs to start looking for a job. Isn't that right, Clint?"

Clint ducked his head. "Yes, Mama. I'll get right on that first thing next week."

Kaylee's phone vibrated in her pocket. She pulled it out. A text message from Allie: *Where are you? Thought you were coming to dinner with us.*

"Oh, crap," she said. "I have to go. Thanks for talking to me." She turned to Mama C. "When can I come back? I have some follow-up questions for you if that's okay."

"That's okay. Stop by tomorrow, chances are we'll still be here." The old woman raised an eyebrow. "Might be nice if you'd bring some food to share with the group."

"Yes, yes. Of course." Kaylee chastised herself for not thinking of that. "See you tomorrow."

CHAPTER 7

"It's about time!" Allie yelled out as Kaylee made her way to their table.

Kaylee's face burned as servers and customers looked at her. Allie had never been a good judge of just how far her voice could carry. But, from the smirk on her face, Kaylee thought she'd known this time. She knew how easily Kaylee got embarrassed.

Max smiled and shook his head before turning to Allie and signing, "*Stop embarrassing her*."

Sliding into the booth across from them, Kaylee caught her friend's twinkling eyes and showed her the first sign language gesture she'd ever learned—it wasn't exactly an ASL approved sign, but it got the point across with just the use of a single finger.

"Where have you been?" Allie asked with a laugh.

"Working on my thesis project."

"Of course. Aren't you supposed to let me or Max know when you're going into the dangerous parts of town? You promised, remember?"

"I thought I told you," Kaylee stammered. "You must have forgotten."

Allie tapped a finger to the side of her head. "This mind is like a steel trap. Once something goes in, it never lets go. Try again."

Kaylee sighed. "Fine. I forgot to tell you. I guess I should tell you I'm going down there again tomorrow."

"Are you all done with finals, then?" Max asked.

"Yes, thank goodness."

A male server stepped up to the table and smiled at Kaylee. "I'm glad you made it, your friends were starting to worry. Can I get you something to drink?"

"I'll have water with lemon, please."

"Okay. Are you all ready to order?"

They ordered, and when the server walked away, Max asked, "How are things going with your thesis project?"

"Slow but good. I made some progress breaking into the inner circle today. I have a feeling the hardest story to get is going to be Mama C's. Most of her crew seem more than willing to talk about themselves."

"You might have to take off your interviewer hat and put on your investigator hat." Allie took a sip of her Diet Coke.

"Yeah." Kaylee looked down at the table. "I might have to."

"Pizza and breadsticks." Kaylee handed the hot pizza box to Demarcus then shrugged a shoulder and smiled at Mama C. "I brought some fruit and canned goods, too, for later."

Mama C took the bags from her, her eyebrows forming a V as she studied Kaylee. "Thank you."

Kaylee looked around, a small heartbeat of disappointment fluttered when she didn't see Blayne among the group.

Mama C chuckled. "He'll be around shortly. I sent him on an errand."

"I...uh...I wasn't..." Heat rushed up her face in stark contrast to the freezing air.

"Of course you weren't." Mama C laughed again. "Let's eat and then you can start grilling me with your questions."

The older woman looked around at Demarcus, Hannah, and Clint. "Who's saying grace?"

"I will, Mama C." Hannah glanced at Kaylee with a look of defiance.

The group moved away from the fire barrel and held hands in a circle, Mama C grabbed Kaylee's hand on one side and Clint grabbed her other one. Kaylee bowed her head slightly like the others, but as they closed their eyes, she squinted out at them.

"Heavenly Father," Hannah began, "we're thankful for this food we're about to eat. Please keep us safe and help us be strong. Amen."

Kaylee said "amen" a heartbeat behind everyone else as she was a little lost in her thoughts. *What do these people have to be thankful for? They're homeless. No family to help them.*

As if she'd read her mind, Mama C looked at Kaylee with a raised eyebrow. "Yes, Miss Kaylee, even those of us on the streets have much to be thankful for." She handed Kaylee a slice of pizza and then took one for herself. "For one," she took a large bite and continued talking as she chewed, "I'm thankful that you have good taste in pizza. Pepperoni, it's the only way to go. If you'd have shown up here with pineapple on this pizza, our little interviews would have been over." She smiled and winked.

Kaylee laughed and took a bite of her slice. Returning to her previous thoughts, she decided she'd been wrong—about a couple of things. They did have a family, they'd made one out of this ragtag group of misfits, all thanks to the strong, strict, laughing woman standing at her side. Kaylee had to know her story. More than just for her thesis project, her investment had grown deeper than that. What made Mama C who she was? She had to find out. She took another bite and chewed thoughtfully. If Mama C wouldn't crack to her questioning today, she'd take Allie's advice and go into investigator mode.

"Save a couple of slices for Blayne." Mama C broke through Kaylee's train of thought.

Kaylee finished her slice of pizza, wiped her hands on a napkin, and threw it in the fire.

Mama C wiped her mouth on her sleeve and nodded to Kaylee. "Okay. Let's get this interview over with."

They moved off to the side, near the slanting wall that rose up to the bridge above, and sat across from each other on five-gallon buckets.

Kaylee took a deep breath and looked the older woman in the eyes. "What's your name?"

Mama C raised an eyebrow and leaned in. "I'm pretty sure I already told you it's Claire."

Looking down at her hands, Kaylee said, "I was hoping you'd maybe tell me your last name, too."

She straightened up and grunted. "Why are you so intent on knowing my last name? It makes no difference to you or your paper."

"I don't know. I guess I'm just wondering why it's important to you to keep it a secret." Kaylee looked up at her and shrugged, smiling to soften the words. "What are you trying to hide?"

A flash of sorrow passed through her eyes. "I'm not trying to hide anything. I just want to keep my past in the past. Some things are better left to lie. Sometimes dredging up the past only serves to increase pain and sorrow." She shook her head. "Bringing those deeply buried memories to the surface can crush a scarred and crippled soul."

The others had all wandered off after eating. Kaylee was thankful for that. Thankful they weren't there to see Mama C's words bring tears to her eyes. She swallowed, determined to continue in a soft voice. "Okay. No last name. Will you tell me where you came from? Are you from Colorado?"

"I am not from Colorado," she said with finality, closing the door on that line of questioning.

"How did you get here?"

"By bus."

That was a tiny bit of information to go off of. "Do you have any family that might be worried about you?"

"No. And again, you are wandering into dangerous territory. Where are you going with this line of questioning? Why is it vital for your thesis?"

"I just feel like your background is important in order to explore why you're so special. What makes you who you are. Like, where do you get your money from? You buy food and things for these kids, but I've never seen you panhandling." Kaylee wrung her hands in her lap.

"Another thing that's none of your business. You're walking a tight rope here, Miss Kaylee. I am who I am. Helping and loving others has always been a part of my soul. None of those things came about because of the misfortunes in my life. In fact, I think the important thing for you to note, is that those things—love and caring —remained a part of my life *in spite* of what went on in my past." Mama C's eyes lifted to gaze above Kaylee's head and a smile touched the corners of her mouth. "Blayne. I'm glad you made it back. We saved a couple slices of pizza for you."

"Uh, thanks." He looked down at Kaylee. "Can I talk to you for a minute, college girl?"

"Umm, sure."

"Over here, Mama doesn't need to hear this." He gestured to a spot fifteen yards away, on the other side of the viaduct.

Kaylee glanced at Mama C then pushed up off the bucket to stand and follow Blayne. When they reached the other side, he spun to face her, eyes narrowed. "What do you think you're doing?"

"I'm...I'm just asking questions for my paper." She wondered how long he'd been within listening distance.

He leaned in closer to her face. "Yeah, questions you aren't supposed to be asking. Questions you promised me you wouldn't ask."

Oh, yeah. She had promised him. "I..." She looked down at her hands. "I'm sorry. She's just so fascinating, I forgot my promise." She raised her head to meet his eyes, but he was no longer looking at her. Following his gaze, she gasped as three dark figures tramped toward them. Blayne pushed her behind him and she looked to where Mama C still sat. Another dark figure approached her, a baseball bat in hand.

"Blayne," she whispered, "Mama C."

He looked her direction and then back at the trouble in front of them. "What do you want?" His voice carried to all four of the intruders.

A shorter guy slapped a tire iron against his hand and stepped forward, the other two flanking him. "We want whatever you got. This looks like a real nice place, too. Protection from the wind, cover from the rain and snow, a nice barrel for fires. Real nice. So, we're gonna take over here for you, too."

"They have food and a coupla' nice sleeping bags over here," yelled the man standing over Mama C.

"We don't want any trouble from you boys." Mama C pushed herself up off the bucket she sat on. "You can have it all. We'll just be on our way." Her voice remained steady with a touch of resignation—as if she was getting tired of the game. As if this had happened too many times to count. "Come on Blayne. Kaylee. Let's leave these boys to it."

The guy with the tire iron perked up and leaned around Blayne. He raised his eyebrows and licked his lips when he saw Kaylee huddled behind him. Blayne's hands curled into fists at his sides and he stepped sideways, blocking the guy's view. "Go collect your spoils. We're leaving," he growled.

Blayne reached behind him and grabbed Kaylee's hand, pulling her after him. Keeping his body between hers and the viaduct pirates. She held tight as her adrenaline kicked in and her pulse skyrocketed.

"Now wait a minute." The guy shoved the tip of the tire iron in Blayne's chest. "What do we have here?"

Blayne stood his ground. One of the guy's cohorts rushed around and grabbed Kaylee's coat, pulling her away from Blayne. The scent of body odor, urine, and alcohol attacked as she drew in a sharp, frightened breath. *Fight or flight,* she thought. She twisted away from his grip on her coat and came face-to-face with the third guy. She slammed her knee into his groin and backed up as he buckled over in pain. Blayne had somehow taken control of the tire iron and wielded it out in front of him.

"Just let us go and you can have everything," Mama C shouted.

"Shut up old lady!" the guy facing off with Blayne yelled. "We found something else we want."

Blayne's eyes flashed anger and his grip tightened on the iron. He swung but didn't connect as the mouthy pig jumped back just in time.

An arm wrapped around Kaylee's neck and a body pressed up against hers from behind. A glint of light reflected off a rusty blade as her assailant pushed the knife against her cheek. "Better back off, Romeo. Drop the tire iron." His rancid breath brushed her face, and she gagged.

Kaylee's eyes met Blayne's for a split second and she knew he wasn't going to drop it. Blayne swung up, catching the shorter man right across the jaw with a crunching blow. In the same motion he slammed the weapon down on the shoulders of the man Kaylee had kneed as he tried to stand. Taking her cue from Blayne, Kaylee pulled down on the arm around her neck with both hands, using all her weight and twisting out of his grasp in time avoid the brunt of Blayne's tackle. The tire iron flew out of his hand and skittered across the gravel as both Blayne and the knife-wielding man crashed to the ground. The blade plunged into Blayne's left shoulder. He grunted and Kaylee's hands flew to her mouth. "Blayne!"

Blayne sat up, straddling the man, and slammed a fist into his face. The knife dropped from his now limp hand and clattered to the ground.

"Blayne!" Mama C shouted.

Guy number four rushed toward them with his bat up and ready to swing. Kaylee jumped and grabbed the tire iron, tripping the man with a swing at his knees. "Let's go! My car!" She held tight to the tire iron in one hand, grabbing Blayne's arm with the other as she urged him to stand. The three of them, Mama C clutching a small duffle bag, hurried to Kaylee's car parked behind a dumpster a dozen yards away. As they neared it, she handed the tire iron to Blayne and reached into her coat pocket for the keys. She pushed the door unlock button twice and risked a glance behind her as she reached for the driver's door handle. The only pursuer was the guy with the bat, but she must have knocked his knee a good one, because he limped along at a much slower pace than even Mama C. Blayne opened the back door and ushered Mama inside, slamming it before running around to the passenger side. He slid in with a grunt and closed the door. Kaylee hit the lock button and tangled with the keys, trying to get the right one in the ignition with her shaky hands.

She started her car and pulled away as the bat flew through the air and bounced off her trunk. She accelerated onto a main road and risked a glance at Blayne. The part of his face she could see between long bangs and facial hair was pale. He reached his hand around to his left shoulder and pulled bloody fingers away.

"I need to get you to the hospital," Kaylee said.

"No."

"But you've been stabbed!" Her stomach lurched.

"It's not that deep. I'll be fine." Blayne leaned his head back.

"How do you know how deep it is?" She met Mama C's gaze in the rearview mirror. "Mama C. Talk some sense into him."

"Blayne," Mama C leaned forward, "maybe she's right."

"I'm fine. No hospital. I don't have insurance or an I.D. or money. We can just go somewhere and clean it up a little."

"None of that matters," Kaylee argued. "They have to see you in the ER, it's a law."

Blayne shook his head. "No, Kaylee." He grimaced as he lifted his left hand to lay it on top of her right. "No hospital."

Kaylee bit her bottom lip. "Okay. But at least let me take you to my roommate's boyfriend. He's a medical student, and I'd just feel better if he took a look at it." She squeezed his hand. "Please."

He closed his eyes and sighed. "Okay. Fine."

"Well, now that that's settled," Mama C Said. "Could you please drop me off downtown, near the shelter. I need to find the other kids before they head back to the viaduct." She turned to look at Blayne. "Meet us there, at the shelter, and we'll find a new place together."

Blayne nodded.

CHAPTER 8

"Which shelter do you want me to drop you at?" Kaylee asked Mama C.

"The one over on Park Ave. Do you know where that is?"

"I think so. It's a few blocks away from Coors Field." Kaylee pulled her phone out of her pocket and held in the home button before saying, "Call Allie." She held the phone up to her ear as she turned onto Broadway. "Hey, Allie. Um, what are you and Max up to?"

She waited while Allie's app translated her speech into text.

"Nothing much. We're at Max's place. He's studying and I'm watching T.V. Why?"

"I'm, uh..." she glanced at Blayne then back at the road, "bringing a friend over that needs some medical care. Maybe stitches."

Pause.

"Is it that hot homeless guy?" Allie said it loud enough that Kaylee was sure Mama C and Blayne both heard her.

"Be there in about fifteen minutes. Bye." Kaylee hit "end" before Allie could say anything else. Heat rushed up her neck and face as she concentrated on the road ahead.

She pulled up to the curb in front of the shelter. Blayne got out, wincing as he did, and helped Mama C out of the back seat. "I'll come find you here when I get done. Stay safe."

Mama C patted his face and smiled a sad smile. "I will. You cooperate with Kaylee's friend. I need you to be okay."

He nodded as she stepped up onto the sidewalk. He slid back in, glancing at the blood on the backrest of the passenger seat. "Sorry about the blood."

Kaylee rolled her eyes. "I'm not worried about my seat, Blayne." She turned to face him. "Are you sure Mama C is going to be okay here?" Her eyes flicked to the rough-looking men and women loitering around the shelter.

"She's just as safe here as anywhere else. But she'll be a lot safer when I get back to watch over her." He looked pointedly into her eyes.

With a big sigh, Kaylee put the car in drive and pulled out onto the road.

Allie met them at the door to Max's apartment with a smile. "You must be Blayne. I'm Kaylee's friend, Allie. Come on in."

Blayne raised an eyebrow at Kaylee and followed Allie inside. Allie gestured to a couch and said, "Have a seat. I'll go get Max."

"Oh," Blayne said. "I don't want to get your couch dirty. Or bloody. I'll just stand, thank you."

Allie crinkled her forehead and opened her mouth, she turned to Kaylee and signed.

Looking from one to the other, Blayne stammered, "I...oh...is she...is she *deaf*? I didn't know."

"It's okay." Kaylee laughed nervously. "I should have told you. She is really great at reading lips, but she can't read yours because your facial hair is in the way."

He reached up and stroked his beard. "Sorry," he mumbled.

"Let's go in the kitchen," Kaylee said. She led them to the small kitchen area and pulled a chair out, gesturing for Blayne to sit there. "Let me help you take your coat off."

"I can get it." Blayne unzipped his coat and shrugged his shoulders, wincing.

"Oh, just let me help." Kaylee tugged gently on the sleeves, pulling the coat off. She hung it on the back of the chair.

"Thanks."

Max entered the kitchen, carrying a medical bag, and held his hand out to Blayne. "I'm Max. It's nice to meet you."

After a slight moment of hesitation, Blayne pulled the tattered glove off his right hand and shook hands with Max. "I'm Blayne. Thanks for helping me out."

"You're welcome." He looked Blayne over. "Where is the injury?"

Blayne pointed over his left shoulder. "Back there."

"Let's get these shirts off so I can take a look." Max moved around to the back of the chair.

It took a few minutes for Blayne to remove the button-down flannel shirt and three T-shirts beneath. Kaylee stepped forward to help, but stopped at the narrow-eyed look he gave her. She backed up and stood silently behind him.

Allie grabbed the pile of worn shirts and his coat. "I'm just going to throw these in the washer for you." She didn't wait for a response—she rarely did.

"But..." Blayne turned to watch her bounce down the hallway. "I'm kinda in a hurry," he mumbled under his breath.

Max laughed. "Even if she could hear you, she'd still ignore you. That girl has a mind of her own." He pulled a chair over behind Blayne and fished some gloves out of his bag, snapping them as he fit them over his fingers. "Let's take a look at this laceration."

Blayne gritted his teeth as Max poked around the injury.

"How did this happen?" Max pulled the gloves off and dug around in his bag.

"He was—" Kaylee started.

"I fell," Blayne interrupted. "Landed on a sharp piece of metal."

Max raised an eyebrow but didn't question any further. "Well, it definitely needs sutures, and you'll need a tetanus shot. I'm going to numb it up before I clean it out. This is going to sting."

Kaylee winced and turned away, suddenly finding the pattern on the counter-top to be fascinating.

Clouds covered the light of the stars and moon as Kaylee pulled up to the shelter. She didn't know how Max had gotten his hands on a tetanus shot, but she was glad he had. Besides being rusty, that knife likely had some other deadly germs on it. The wound took six stitches and luckily wasn't very deep. They'd all sat around talking when Max was done, while they waited for Blayne's coat and shirts to dry. Max gave Blayne a t-shirt to wear while they waited.

"Do you want me to help you find Mama C?" Kaylee asked as she put the car in park.

"No. I know where they'll be." He opened the door. "Thanks for everything. You have some great friends."

She smiled. "I do."

He hesitated. "Well, see you around." He moved to get out of the car.

"Wait!" Kaylee grasped his arm. "How am I going to know where to find you?"

Blayne sat back in the seat and frowned. "I had hoped that the events of tonight had convinced you of the danger of hanging out around us. Are you seriously going to keep this up? Don't you have enough information for your paper?"

A lump formed in Kaylee's throat. She swallowed it down. Did she have enough information? Why did she so desperately want to continue this quest? Was it to learn more about Mama C? Or more about Blayne? She stared at his cool blue eyes. "I don't have enough yet. I...I need to do some more observation." *And this is more than just a thesis paper now.*

"Hmm." He looked away from her gaze. "It might take us a day or so to find a new place. I'll meet you back here day after tomorrow. Noonish."

Kaylee smiled and squeezed his arm. "Thank you!"

"Mmff," he grunted. Kaylee thought she saw just the hint of a smile hiding beneath his mustache. Just a hint. He didn't look back at her as he shut the door and trudged off to find Mama and the others.

As she unlocked her door and stepped into her warm apartment, a wave of guilt washed over her. Mama C, Blayne, and the others didn't know where they'd be sleeping tonight. Their sleeping bags were gone. It was below freezing out there.

She shut the door behind her, then slumped to the floor. The tears came hard and fast—and unexpected. She cried out of fear for her new friends. She cried for the chilling experience with the thieves that night. She cried for the unfairness of the world. And, mostly, she cried because she felt so helpless to do anything to change it.

CHAPTER 9

Christmas had snuck up on Kaylee. As she wandered through the mall with Allie, Christmas music playing throughout the decorated stores, she realized it was December 22nd already. She stopped at a kiosk and looked at the portable media players. She picked one up and turned it over before quickly setting it back down. Way too much money for her meager budget.

Allie sidled up alongside her. "Don't buy that. I have a brand new one that you can have." She grabbed Kaylee's hand and pulled her away. "Let's go check out the big shoe sale."

"Wait." Kaylee pulled on Allie's hand to stop her mad dash through the crowded mall. Allie turned to face her. "Why do *you* have a media player?"

Allie's mouth twisted up into a grin. "I got it for free when I opened my bank account."

Kaylee laughed and shook her head. "Are you sure you want to give it to me? Maybe someone in your family could use it."

"Nope, I want you to have it. It's still in the package. It comes with earbuds and everything." The conversation ended when Allie turned away from Kaylee and dragged her forward into the crowd.

After visiting several second-hand stores to buy some sleeping bags, Kaylee spent the rest of the day holed up in her room, downloading music, thankful she'd saved the multiple gift cards she'd received for birthdays and Christmases.

The next day, she loaded up her car with the sleeping bags, grabbed some five-dollar pizzas, and headed to the shelter where Blayne said he'd meet her. The winter sun shone bright, beating away some of the chill, as she pulled up to the same section of sidewalk where she'd dropped him off two days ago. She checked to make sure her doors were locked, then sat in her warm car watching the people gathered on the sidewalks there. Two men and a woman fighting over a shopping cart; a man slumped over, back against the brick building, a shivering dog lying next to him; a woman half hidden under a threadbare blanket, injecting drugs into her scabbed and scarred arm; men and women drinking out of bottles hidden in paper bags. Mama C and her group seemed downright put-together compared to these people. *They used to be these people, though—until Mama found them.*

A sharp *rap* on her window startled her, and she whipped her head around to see a mischievous grin on Blayne's face. She scowled at him and motioned for him to go around to the passenger seat as she unlocked the doors.

He slid in and shut the door. "Whew. It's warm in here. It was a cold night without any sleeping bags."

Kaylee's gaze fell to her lap. "I bet it was. Did you guys find somewhere to...to stay?"

"We did. Head that way and I'll show you." He pointed straight ahead.

She pulled out into the street. "How is your shoulder doing?"

"It's fine. The arm where he gave me the tetanus shot hurts worse." He rolled his shoulder. "Do I smell pizza?" He looked in the back seat.

"Yes, you do. Do you want a piece now or do you want to wait until we get to the others?"

"I'll wait." His stomach disagreed loudly with a growl.

He directed her to a bridge a couple of miles away from the shelter. Weeds and scrub bushes lightly covered in snow dotted the area beneath the bridge. No barrel for a fire here. Kaylee frowned.

She popped the trunk and reached into the backseat to grab the pizza. "Can you help me grab some stuff from my trunk, please?"

"Umm, sure." He raised an eyebrow at her before getting out of the car. He met her at the trunk. "What is all this?"

"I just picked some stuff up from some second-hand stores. Think of it as an early Christmas present for Mama C's gang." She didn't look at him, afraid he wouldn't appreciate her gifts. She knew he didn't like to be pitied.

"Hmm. That was very thoughtful of you."

She dared a glance at him, surprised to see sincerity mixed with a touch of—confusion, maybe?—in his eyes. "It's just some sleeping bags and blankets and stuff." She couldn't tear her eyes away from his. He broke first.

"Well," he cleared his throat and reached for one of the bundles in the trunk, "let's get these over there, get Mama C warmed up."

The smaller package tucked away in her coat pocket would have to wait until later. She balanced the pizzas in one hand and grabbed a sleeping bag with the other and set out to follow Blayne over to the small group.

As they neared the new encampment, Mama C stood and smiled. "You three go help carry that stuff. College girl looks like she's going to drop those pizzas right into the dirt."

Demarcus and Clint strode forward and took the items from her. Hannah stood slowly, shrugged, and said, "It looks like they got it all."

"There's more in the trunk if you want to come help me get it," Kaylee said.

Hannah sighed and trudged toward her.

Altogether, Kaylee scraped together five sleeping bags and a couple of old quilts. Mama C grabbed her hands after she dropped her last load. "Kaylee, sweetie, thank you so much. These will be lifesavers for us."

Kaylee squeezed her hands and whispered, "Merry Christmas, Mama C."

The old woman furrowed her brow. "Is it Christmas already?"

Kaylee laughed nervously. "No, but almost. Today is the twenty-third. I didn't think you'd want to wait two more days for a little warmth."

"Oh boy, you're right there. We're sure missing our barrel o' fire."

The others had already started on the pizza. Kaylee and Mama walked over to them and each grabbed a slice. "Sorry it's pizza again," Kaylee said with a shrug. "It's cheap, and it feeds a lot of people."

Demarcus straightened up and pointed a finger at her in mock consternation. "Don't ever let me hear you apologize for pizza again. Pizza is a national treasure!" As if to prove it, he shoved half a piece into his mouth and smiled a marinara-cheesy smile.

When the pizza was gone, the three teens and Mama wrapped up in the sleeping bags and Kaylee draped one of the quilts over her legs as she sat on a flat stone. Mama C pulled her beanie down over her ears and said, "Well, are you going to ask me more questions today, college girl?"

Kaylee glanced at Blayne, still standing in front of them, then back at Mama. "Not today. Today is just for hanging out."

Mama C smiled and nodded.

"I'm gonna go see if I can find something to burn," Blayne said. "Be back in a few."

Kaylee jumped to her feet and spread the quilt over Mama C. "I'll come with you."

Blayne shrugged and turned his back to her. "If you want, I guess."

A low chuckle came from Mama's throat.

Kaylee caught up to him, her face flushed yet again.

"You really wanna go dumpster diving with me?"

"Umm, yeah. Is that where you find wood?"

"Sometimes. Not far from here there's some abandoned buildings with boarded-up windows. That's actually where I'm headed this time."

They walked in silence for a few minutes until the buildings came into view. "Might need to go inside and scope it out. That wood looks soaked." Blayne stopped and looked down at Kaylee. "You okay with a little breaking and entering, college girl?"

She shrugged. "It wouldn't be the first time."

His eyes widened. "Oh, really? Do tell."

The pert little twist of his lips was worth the confession. "Okay. But this stays between us. I don't need everyone else finding out about my checkered past." She put her hands on her hips in a dramatic fashion.

Blayne laughed and crossed his heart. "Your secret shall go to the grave with me."

"Back home, there was this old, abandoned house. Everyone said it was haunted. We'd dare each other to go look through the only window that wasn't boarded up."

"Ooh. Scary." He rolled his eyes.

"Oh, it gets better." Kaylee crossed her arms. "One Halloween—I think I was fifteen—this older boy I had a secret crush on, who turned out to be a real jerk, by the way, dared me to go inside the house. Said he'd give me something really special if I did."

Blayne's eyes narrowed. "Special, huh?"

"Yeah," Kaylee scoffed. "Like I said—a real jerk."

"So, did you do it?"

"Of course I did! I'm no scaredy-cat. I took a hammer and pulled enough boards off one of the back windows to climb through. I flipped on my flashlight and heard hundreds of little feet skittering." She shuddered at the memory. "The dare was that I had to walk to the front of the house and shine the flashlight out of the non-boarded-up window, take something from inside, then go back out the way I came in. I covered my mouth with my shirt and stepped carefully over dead rodents and spider webs until I could shine the light out the window. On the way back out I noticed an old key hanging from a hook in the kitchen. I grabbed that and booked it out of there."

"So, breaking, entering, *and* robbery." He nodded. "I'm impressed, college girl."

"I still have the key somewhere."

"As you should. You should always keep mementos of your crimes, I mean, adventures."

She smiled up at him. The sparkle in his eyes lit a fire in her chest. She reached into her pocket and felt the package there. "I... uh...I have something for you. A thank you for, well, for helping me out." She pulled the wrapped package out and handed it to him, the fire moving up her neck into her face.

A slight frown creased his brow.

Words tumbled out of her. "It's no big deal, really. I didn't even have to buy it. Allie gave it to me. I just thought you might like it."

He sighed and took it from her. "Thank you."

She watched as he unwrapped the small media player. He held it up and raised an eyebrow.

She hurried to explain. "I downloaded some songs I think you'll like. It's all charged up, and it comes with earbuds and a charging cord." She looked down. "I figured you could probably find places to plug it in and recharge it, or I could recharge it for you."

A strange look passed over his face. "So, you plan on sticking around long enough to recharge this for me?" Unlike other times, he didn't sound put-off or annoyed. He sounded almost—hopeful.

"Yeah. I do." She reached up and squeezed his hand. "Maybe it was a dumb idea. I've never been good at giving gifts." She let her hand drop.

"Kaylee," he waited for her to look up at him before continuing, "It's a wonderful gift. Will you show me how it works? I've been a bit tech-deprived for a while."

She nodded, unable to tear her gaze from his. There was something in his eyes she'd never seen there before—like the ice around his heart was slowly melting and maybe he was seeing her as something besides a spoiled college girl. "That's the first time you've called me by my name."

Blayne's lips twitched, and he looked away. "Don't make this awkward, college girl."

"Right." She nodded. "Let's find somewhere to sit while I show you how it works."

Glad for her long coat that covered her butt, they sat on a bench that was more splinters than boards. Blayne pulled the media player out of the box and scooted closer to her, so their legs touched. Kaylee removed her gloves so she could work the touch-screen, wondering at the odor of freshly laundered clothing.

As if reading her mind, Blayne leaned closer, holding out the player to her. "Don't worry. I took advantage of the showers and laundering facilities at the shelter the other day. I should be bug and mostly odor free."

"You do smell nice. I mean fresh." She growled and shook her head like a confused pup. She let out a deep breath. "You smell clean, and I'm sure it felt good to take a warm shower and put on clean clothes."

Blayne chuckled. "You really aren't very good at the whole conversation thing, are you?"

Not with you, she thought. "Things always sound better in my head. Something happens on the way to my mouth, so by the time the words get there, they're all screwed up."

He caught on quickly to her tutorial, and she wondered whether it was her fabulous teaching or that he actually already knew how to work it. Either way, it didn't matter, each time their hands brushed against one another, or he looked at her and smiled, her stomach released another butterfly into her chest. She could no longer deny it —she was attracted to a recovering drug addict homeless guy. She frowned at the thought. What was she doing?

CHAPTER 10

Snowflakes floated down in a half-hearted attempt at a storm. Kaylee stared out at the gray street from Max's apartment window, trying to keep her mind from wandering to Blayne. It was Christmas Day, though, so was it so weird for her to wonder how Mama C and her gang were doing?

Allie plopped down next to her on the loveseat and she turned from the window with a start.

"Sorry," Allie said, not looking at all sorry. "I made you some hot chocolate."

"Thank you." Kaylee took the steaming mug from her friend.

"Lame Christmas, huh?" Allie brushed a stray hair from her face. "Maybe you should have gone home."

Kaylee smiled. "It isn't lame. I appreciate you and Max letting me spend the day with you. And eat dinner with you." She rubbed her stomach with exaggerated strokes. "When did you say we'd be eating?"

"Max says the turkey should be done soon. He's just waiting for the little temp probe thing to pop up."

"You know those things don't always work, right?" Kaylee raised an eyebrow.

"Um, no, I didn't know that." She stood and rushed to the kitchen.

The turkey ended up being dry, but still good. Max and Allie packed up all the leftovers—of which there were many, making Kaylee wonder if they'd purposefully bought a bigger turkey and more food than they would need—and told Kaylee to take it, and do "whatever she wanted" with it. They really weren't as sneaky as they thought.

The door let in a chilling breeze and a few random snowflakes as they said their goodbyes. "It's getting kind of late," Allie said. "Maybe we should go with you."

"It isn't late," Kaylee said. "It just looks that way because the days are so short this time of year." She patted Allie's hand. "I'll be fine. Thank you again for dinner, and the leftovers." She would have liked their company but was afraid it would upset the group she'd worked so hard to gain trust from if she brought a couple of strangers in their midst. *Besides, Blayne will keep me safe.* She scowled at herself for thinking of him again.

Kaylee stopped at her and Allie's apartment to gather some paper plates and plastic utensils. She thought about just stopping to buy some at a gas station, but money was tight, especially during school breaks when she wasn't TA-ing. She wouldn't see another paycheck until a couple of weeks after school started again in mid-January. The money her parents and grandparents sent her for Christmas would help get her by.

The gang huddled around a pitiful excuse for a fire under the new viaduct. Blayne stood off from them, hands in his pockets, watching Mama C from behind. She was wrapped up in two sleeping bags and wore a beanie, a scarf wrapped around her face so only her dark eyes were visible.

Kaylee cleared her throat to get their attention. "I brought left-overs."

The teens perked up, lifting their gazes from the hypnotic flames. "Let me help you with that," Demarcus said, jumping to his feet. Clint was right behind him.

Even Hannah stood and moved toward her. "Pizza again?"

Kaylee smiled. "Not this time. Turkey dinner. If you hurry, it might actually still be warm."

"Mashed potatoes?" Demarcus licked his lips.

"Yep. And gravy." Kaylee and the boys spread the plastic food containers out on the ground near the fire and then Kaylee passed out the plates and utensils.

Blayne leaned down, put a hand on her shoulder, and whispered in her ear. "This is really great. Thank you."

His warm breath sent a shiver down her back. "You're welcome," she whispered in return.

After they devoured all of the leftovers, they sat around the fire. Blayne sat close to Kaylee, their shoulders brushing as he leaned in to tend to the fire. Mama C sat on the other side of her. The silence lingered, but didn't feel awkward as they all stared at the flames, lost in their own thoughts.

"What's your favorite Christmas memory, Demarcus?" Clint asked, breaking the silence.

Demarcus glanced around the circle, then looked up, thinking. "I guess, the year before my mom got sick. That was the last Christmas we were all together. The last time we had a nice Christmas dinner." He winked at Kaylee.

"What about you Hannah?" Clint asked.

"Oh, when I was ten, my grandma and grandpa rented a cabin in the mountains for us to spend the holidays in. It was awesome. My cousins were there, and we stayed up and played games every night. We had a massive snowball fight, kids against grown-ups, and we had the advantage because we'd spent the morning building a snow fort to hide behind." She sighed. "It was awesome."

"Blayne?" Clint raised his eyebrows at his friend sitting across from him.

Blayne shook his head.

"Come on! Tell us something," Clint pleaded. "Lie if you have to."

Blayne laughed and glanced quickly at Kaylee then back at the flames. "This one has turned out to be pretty nice."

Looking down at her lap, Kaylee smiled to herself.

"That's a cop-out," Clint said. "But whatever. Your turn, college girl."

"You go first, Clint," she stalled.

"Fine, but then you have to go." He rubbed his hands together and smiled. "We went ice skating on a pond my dad used to skate on as a kid. It was terrifying, because the ice makes noise and I was sure we were going to fall through and die a horrible, frozen death. But it was also exhilarating. Me and my sister chased my dad around, trying to get him to fall while my mom laughed and tried to keep up with us. It was a blast.

"Your turn." He smiled and nodded at Kaylee.

She groaned. "Do I have to take a turn?"

"Yes, ma'am."

"This is embarrassing, but my favorite Christmas was when I was about eight and my grandma got me a karaoke machine."

Everyone laughed.

Kaylee hurried to explain. "But not because of the present. It was my favorite because my whole family, reluctantly at first, had a sing-off. Even my usually stoic dad. It was awful, and hilarious, and so much fun. I don't think I've ever laughed so hard in my life."

She turned to Mama C. "How about you, Mama C?"

The others quieted and looked back at the flames.

"You know I don't talk about my past, Kaylee." She coughed, holding a gloved hand to her mouth. "But I do want to raise your awareness of something." She looked around at the gathered group as she spoke. "Not a single one of you talked about *things* when talking about your favorite Christmas. Not one of you talked about a favorite present. You all referred to spending time with those you love. That is what's important. That is what we remember as we lay dying. That is what we yearn for again when we're lonely and alone. And, that is what some folks cry themselves to sleep wishing for when even the possibility of such a thing is buried in the past, impossible to obtain. Feel fortunate, my young ones, that the *possibility* is still there for all of you." She wiped away a tear, no longer looking at anyone, but gazing into the fire.

Kaylee laid her hand atop Mama C's gloved hand. "But there must be *someone* you'd like to see again."

"No." Mama C's voice turned harsh. "You won't trick me into talking about my past. Stop trying."

Blayne bristled on Kaylee's other side. "I think it's time for you to go now, college girl." He stood and held a hand out to help her up, not leaving it open for discussion.

"I'm sorry," she whispered to Mama C as she stood.

"I'll walk you to your car." The light had gone out of Blayne's voice too. Her incessant curiosity had ruined a beautiful night, and she was furious with herself.

"Wait," Mama C struggled to stand, another dry cough roughing up her throat. "I'd like to have a word with you, Kaylee," she narrowed her eyes at Blayne, "alone."

Kaylee and the elderly woman stepped out of hearing range from Blayne and the group. Kaylee barley held back tears, knowing Mama C would tell her she could no longer come around. Knowing she'd blown it.

A gentle smile softened her eyes, though, and Mama said, "There is something I'd like you to do. Consider it making up for your repeated breaking of my rules—which you agreed to."

Relief washed over her and Kaylee nodded. "Yes. Anything."

Placing a hand on Kaylee's arm, Mama C said, "I want you to help Blayne. He's ready to leave this life behind. He's been ready for a while now."

Confused, Kaylee asked, "How can I help him?"

"First of all, he needs a job. There are programs out there that can help with this, but they take some time to complete and I don't think he needs that. But there are things that are necessary in order to even apply for a job, things Blayne does not have access to."

Kaylee waited for her to continue, hoping she wasn't going to ask her for money, because that was one thing she was unable to give right now.

"Clothes. He needs some decent clothes and I don't mean for you to buy them for him. There are several places—churches and shelters —that have free, donated clothing for just such a purpose, but he'll need to be able to get to those places. And he'll need help picking out the proper attire.

"A haircut and shave. Again, not asking you to pay for it. Those same places that supply clothing, have barbers come and give of their time and talents for free on certain days of the week or month. Find out when and get him there."

So far, the list seemed doable.

Mama C continued, "And, this is the hard one, he'll need to get a copy of his Social Security Card. He knows his number, but employers need a copy of an actual card. I have no idea what is needed to get it. I have a feeling it won't be easy without an I.D. or permanent address. You'll have to do some research into that."

Kaylee nodded again, already thinking of ways she could find out. "He can use my phone number to put on the applications and I can drive him to any interviews he gets."

"Now," Mama C said, "the hard part is up to me." She patted Kaylee's arm. "I get to convince him to let you help."

CHAPTER 11

Downtown Denver bustled with people and cars. Kaylee thought it would have settled down a few days after Christmas, but people must have still been out visiting family and exchanging unwanted or mis-sized gifts. The traffic tried her patience. It didn't help that she was having little luck with the Social Security Card mission. It was a catch-22—Blayne would need an I.D. or birth certificate to get a copy of his SSC, but he needed his SSC plus two forms of mail to prove his address in order to get an I.D. She was on her way to the homeless shelter to talk to someone whose job it was to deal with these kinds of conundrums. She may have also been using this task as an excuse to postpone going to find Blayne. Mama C had been able to talk him into letting Kaylee help him, but he wasn't happy about it.

She drove around the block twice trying to find a place to park before giving up and parking three blocks away. She wrapped her scarf tighter around her face and neck to ward off the bitter cold. Knowing she shouldn't be walking with her head down, she did it anyway. All of the self-defense classes she'd seen said to walk with purpose, head up and alert. Kaylee had a hard time looking at the people huddled in doorways and out on the sidewalk. She wanted to help them, but had no idea where to even start.

She entered through the main doors of the Denver Rescue Mission and headed straight to the information desk, unwrapping her scarf as she walked. "I have an appointment with Hope Williams."

The woman at the desk smiled. "I'll walk you to her office. This place is a maze if you don't know your way around."

"So," Kaylee tried to hide her annoyance, but she wasn't doing a good job. "I was right, then. There's no way for a homeless person with no contact with his family to get a copy of his Social Security Card. You realize this makes it nearly impossible for someone to get out of the situation they're in, right?"

Hope, the Case Manager Kaylee was meeting with, leaned forward across her desk. "Yes, Ms. Burke, I do realize it. This is one of the many battles I face every day."

"And there's no way around it?"

"Not that I've found in my five years of working here. Your friend is going to have to contact his family. Or you'll have to do it for him."

Gravel crunched under her feet as Kaylee made her way to the encampment under the viaduct, in no hurry to face a probable ornery Blayne. She most definitely wasn't going to tell him what she'd found out about getting a Social Security Card—not today, anyway.

She smiled warily as Blayne straightened from leaning on a cement pillar and walked toward her. The expected scowl did not adorn his face, but his eyebrows scrunched a little as he closed in on her.

"You really don't have to do this, college girl. I can do this myself."

"I...I know. But it'll be faster with me driving you." Kaylee peeked behind him, of course Mama C was nowhere to be found to help her in this conversation.

"Don't you have anything better to do? I'd hate to keep you from your classes."

Did he mean that or was he mocking her? She really couldn't tell. "I'm between semesters. I don't start again until mid-January. So, to answer your question, I don't have anything better to do."

"Don't you have a job? Or do your parents pay your way?" Ahh, there was the snark she expected from him.

Her anger flared just a touch. She swallowed it down and replied. "No, my parents don't support me. I pay for college with scholarships and I work as a TA when school is in session. But, like I said, it's between semesters, so no school and no work." She turned and headed back toward her car, only caring a little bit whether he followed her or not.

After a brief pause, footsteps scuffed behind her, hurrying, it seemed, to catch up. He reached her side and, with a gentler voice, said, "So, that means you don't have any money coming in right now."

Kaylee nodded, looking straight ahead.

"And yet, you've been spending money on food and stuff for us." He stopped, grabbing her arm at the elbow, stopping her mid-stride.

She turned to face him, still not able to look him in the eyes.

He dipped his head down a little, his gloved hand touching her chin to lift her face to meet his gaze. "And gas, Kaylee. You're paying for gas to chauffer me around like a privileged asshole or something."

"It's fine."

"No! It isn't fine," he interrupted. "What are you going to do when you run out of money weeks before your job starts up again? And, you will run out—if you haven't already." Ahh, there was the scowl she'd been expecting since pulling up.

She crossed her arms and cocked a hip out—the same stance she used to take when her parents tried to baby her. "I have it covered. You don't need to worry about it."

His expression and his voice softened. "I *do* have to worry about it. I don't want you ending up out here on the streets because of your tender heart. Because of *me*. I can't stand the thought of it."

Kaylee sighed and loosened her rebellious stance. He was right to worry. Like many people, she had little savings and, without the safety net of her family, could easily find herself unable to pay rent. "I have savings I can tap into. And, as a last resort, credit cards." That was a bit of a lie, she'd already tapped into the credit cards.

Blayne shook his head. "I can't...I can't justify this. I don't want to use you like this."

"You aren't using me!" She swallowed, forcing her voice to lower. "You aren't using me, Blayne. I *want* to do this. For Mama C. For you." She bit her bottom lip to keep a tremor at bay then attempted a smile. "Besides, you're keeping me from spending money on stupid things. I tend to go on unnecessary shopping sprees when I get bored between semesters, then spend the next several months paying extra on my credit cards. See, you're actually *saving* me money by allowing me to drive you around like a privileged A-hole."

His mouth quirked, probably because of her pacifying of his language. "You wouldn't lie to me about this, would you?"

"No. Now can we go? We have a lot to do today."

"Fine. But when I get a job, I'm paying you back."

Kaylee rolled her eyes and turned to walk the rest of the way to her car.

She should have waited in her car. But Kaylee had been afraid Blayne would chicken out and leave out a side door or something. Standing room only in the small Catholic shelter, she leaned against the wall, fanning herself with the end of her scarf. She tried not to wince anytime a nauseating odor wafted her way from one of the many unwashed people waiting their turn for the free haircuts. She admired the barbers and hair dressers who donated their time and skills once a week. Blayne had been in there for at least a half hour. They'd gone there first to make sure he got a turn before the barber packed up and left. They'd go to the bigger shelter on Park Avenue to get him some clothes. She'd done some research, and they had the best selection of nicer used clothing for job interviews because of their fresh-start program.

Kaylee focused on her phone as she read through the day's headlines. Vaguely aware that someone had approached her, she didn't look up until they cleared their throat. When she did look up, it took her a minute to recognize him, only fully registering that it was Blayne when her gaze made it to his ice-blue eyes. She dropped her phone. And her jaw.

"Well, what do you think?" he asked, eyebrows creased into a worry line.

As he bent to pick up her phone, Kaylee got control of herself—mostly. She snapped her mouth shut and held her breath for a couple of seconds to try to calm her out-of-control heart.

"Kaylee?"

He held her phone out to her. When she didn't reach for it, he grabbed her hand and lifted it, then set the phone in her palm and curled her fingers around it. Rarely had he touched her without his winter gloves, and the warmth of his skin on her fingers sent her heart into another fit of fluttering.

She wanted to tear her gaze away from his face. Didn't she? No—it was too beautiful. Yes—she was embarrassing herself.

Blayne coughed nervously and looked down. "Weird, huh?"

Snap out of it! "You...umm...you look amazing." She raised her hand, meaning to touch the smooth skin where his beard used to be. She stopped herself just in time, pulling her hand to the back of her neck, pretending she had an itch there.

He smiled. He had a dimple on his left cheek. Kaylee's tenuous control crumbled further. His lips, though chapped, were perfectly formed. In fact, his whole face could have been the model for Da Vinci's perfect face drawing. "Thank you," he said. "It's been a long time since I've had a clean-shaved face. It feels weird."

"It doesn't look weird." She needed to stop talking. What was with the breathy texture of her voice? She cleared her throat. "Yeah, uh, we should go now. We still need to get you some clothes then go over to the unemployment office." She busied herself with zipping up her coat and putting her gloves on as they pushed through the crowded room to the front door.

CHAPTER 12

They were able to find a pair of black slacks in Blayne's size, a striped button-up shirt, a nice tie, and a pair of black dress shoes only a half size too big for him. He took advantage of the facility's showers before changing into the "new" clothes. Kaylee couldn't stop the whoosh of breath from escaping or the smile from forming on her lips as he stepped out into the front reception area where she waited. Her smile turned up even more, and she laughed once before slapping her hand to her mouth as her gaze landed on his newly cut hair. He had at least tried to comb it, she'd give him that.

He shrugged a shoulder and grinned somewhat sheepishly as he approached her with an outstretched hand holding a cheap plastic comb. "Help." He dropped the bag containing his old clothes on the ground next to her.

Unable to hold it in any longer, Kaylee laughed. "There's nothing wrong with the way you combed your hair, as long as you were going for the Charlie Chaplin look." Another round of laughter as she took the comb from him.

He rolled his eyes as she stretched up on her tippy-toes to better reach his hair. Lowering her arms, she said, "It might be easier if you stoop down or sit on a chair."

He sat in a nearby chair. After just a few strokes of the comb, Kaylee shook her head and handed it back to Blayne. "I think this will work better without the comb, and without the part." She wiggled her fingers through his dark, wet hair. The slight waviness and short cut of it made it the perfect candidate for the "messy" look, even without any hair product to put in it.

She realized she'd been running her fingers through his hair for far longer than necessary, yet she continued to do so for several more seconds. She looked down and her heart fluttered. Blayne's head was tilted slightly up, his eyes closed, and his face more relaxed than she'd ever seen it. She had the sudden strong impulse to lean down and kiss him. She shook her head and pulled her hands away, standing straight and stepping back.

Blayne's eyes opened lazily and searched for hers. "You could keep doing that for, like, an hour if you want." His smile lit up his eyes and his words made her fingers tingle with the desire to run them through his hair again.

She swallowed. Her salivary glands seemed to be working overtime just now. Afraid to speak, she rolled her eyes and crossed her arms. She'd known from his beautiful eyes that he had the potential to be cute—but she was completely taken aback by his movie star looks. She chided herself for thinking such shallow thoughts, but deep inside, she knew she'd felt some sort of attraction to him for a while before this physical transformation.

"Okay, okay." Blayne stood. "I get it. We need to go to the unemployment office now. Do I look presentable?"

Kaylee inhaled sharply and sucked some over-produced saliva into her lungs. A coughing fit of disastrous proportions ensued. The ugly kind—where she couldn't catch her breath, couldn't speak, and, she knew, her face would be bright red, tears spilling from her eyes, and her throat would bulge out like a bullfrog's with each harsh, man-like cough.

To make matters worse, Blayne rushed to her side and threw an arm around her hunched shoulders, causing her already taxed heart to go into overdrive as her skin tingled where he touched her. "Are you okay?" he said. "Can I help? Call an ambulance?"

She shook her head and drew in a breath, which just made the tickling in her throat ten times worse.

"How about a drink of water?" Blayne suggested.

Kaylee nodded, thinking maybe she could get herself together a little while he rushed to get her a drink. She leaned over, propping her hands on her knees, and inhaled, slower this time. She wiped her cheeks, hoping her "waterproof" makeup was truly waterproof.

"Here." Blayne shoved the paper cup of water under her nose.

She straightened up and took another tentative breath before taking the cup from his hand. She took a small sip of the room temperature water. "I think I might have aspiration pneumonia." Her voice came out rough and skipped like a bad-coverage phone call.

Blayne's eyes widened in concern.

"I'm joking, sort of. I'll be fine, everyone chokes on their own saliva sometimes, right?"

"Riiight." He tilted his head. "So, does your reaction mean that I do *not* look presentable?"

She laughed, shaking her head. "No. Just the opposite actually. You look,"—multiple words passed through her brain at the speed of light: amazing, fantastic, devastatingly handsome—"great. Really great."

"You mean now that I don't have Charlie Chaplin hair?"

"Yes. That was definitely not *presentable*." She jerked her head toward the door. "Should we get going?"

He grabbed his bag of old clothes and walked next to her toward the door.

The Colorado Department of Labor and Employment was surprisingly empty compared to the two shelters they'd been to that day. Kaylee sat next to Blayne facing across a desk from a man named Derick.

"Well, Mr. Ellis, at least you know what your Social Security number is. We can at least get you started with that, but if—*when*—you get hired, your employer will need a copy of it before they can pay you." Derrick tapped a pen on the edge of his desk.

"I'm working on that for him," Kaylee said. "Do you have any suggestions on how to get a copy of his card without him having an I.D.?"

They told Derrick about Blayne's situation. He shook his head and looked intently at Blayne. "I'm afraid the only option in this case is for you to contact your parents and see if they can send you either your Social Security Card or your birth certificate."

Blayne sighed and dropped his head, whispering, "I can't do that."

"I can." Kaylee didn't dare look at him. "I'll contact your parents. They can send it to my address."

"No." Blayne continued to bow his head. "I don't want them to know I'm in Denver. I'm not ready."

Kaylee thought for a few seconds. "I'll have them send it to my parents' house in Pueblo and they can forward it to me. I'll explain to your parents that you aren't in Pueblo." She placed her hand on his, which was lying on top of his bouncing knee. "Can I tell them you'll be in contact with them when you're ready?"

He flipped his hand over and curled his fingers tight around hers, still refusing to look up, still bouncing his knee at warp speed. After a pause that seemed to last for hours, he said, "Yeah. Yeah, you can. When I'm back on my feet, I'll call them."

Derrick clapped his hands once. "Well, that's solved." He handed Blayne a paper he'd just printed out. "Now, go over to one of those computers against the wall and enter your information in. The job number on this paper should be the first one you apply to."

"What kind of job is it?" Blayne asked.

"A construction job. They don't care about your past. All they care about is that you show up and work hard and aren't afraid to work in the elements."

Blayne snorted. "Elements I am used to."

Derrick's lips tightened, and he lowered his voice. "That, I'm sure of."

Kaylee wrote her phone number down on a sticky note and handed it to Blayne. "I'll be in the waiting room."

THE DRIVE back to the viaduct was a quiet one. Blayne seemed deep in thought as his leg bounced and he stared out the side window. Kaylee didn't dare interrupt him. As her tires crunched on the gravel that probably wasn't supposed to be used as a road, she turned to him. "It will probably be a few days at least before they call."

"*If* they call," he said.

"They will." She hoped she sounded more confident than she felt. "Maybe you should consider staying at Max's for a few nights, just so I can find you easier if—*when*—someone calls."

He ran his fingers through his hair and shook his head. "No. I don't feel comfortable doing that. I'll stick close to..."

Her ringing phone interrupted him. "Hello?"

The voice on the other end answered, "Hello. Uh, I'm looking for,"—papers shuffled—"Blayne Ellis?"

Kaylee smiled. "He's right here, hold on a second." She handed the phone to a somewhat bewildered Blayne.

His eyes widened as he listened, then he answered, "Yes, ma'am." He glanced at the clock in the car's dash. "Yes, I think I can make it there in a half hour." Listening. "Yes, ma'am, I know where that is." Listening. "Thank you, ma'am. I'll see you shortly."

Missing her hand completely the first time, he handed Kaylee's phone back to her, nearly dropping it the second time, too.

"Well?" she asked.

He turned to face her, a small smile forming at the corners of his mouth. "Can you take me to an interview?"

"Now?"

He nodded and swallowed. "The lady said they need someone that can start right away and my application was the first one she came to that said that."

Shifting the car into reverse, Kaylee did a three-point turn and headed back out to a main road. "Where we going?"

"CU Denver. They have a trailer on site for a construction job there—a business school—she wants to interview me there. I'm hoping you know where that is?"

"I do." She smiled at him and squeezed his hand before concentrating to pull out onto the busy street.

SHE PARKED a couple of buildings away at Blayne's request. Now Kaylee waited impatiently for him to return. He'd been gone for over thirty minutes. She chewed on her nails, a habit she had picked up as a pre-teen. She spit a bit of fingernail toward the steering wheel and cursed under her breath as she surveyed the damage to her thumbnail.

It was an unusually warm day for the end of December, and she sat with the car off and the window cracked just a little to keep the windows from fogging up. She replayed the phone conversation she'd had with Blayne's mom after he'd headed for his interview. The call had been full of tears and thanks. She'd thought for sure her son was dead, buried in some unmarked grave somewhere. She thanked Kaylee over and over and promised to send his birth certificate overnight mail. As badly as she wanted to talk to her son, she understood why he wanted to wait, and told Kaylee to tell him she and his dad and sister love him and couldn't wait to see him again.

She'd taken a break before calling her own mom to tell her to expect the package and send it on to Kaylee ASAP.

"Kaylee!"

She jumped and looked out the windshield. Blayne, big grin on his face, hurried toward her, waving some papers in his hand. She smiled as she threw open the car door and hurried to him. He wrapped his arms around her and lifted her off the ground. "I got the job! I start tomorrow."

He set her down and stared into her eyes. "This would never have happened without your help."

Blood rushed to her head. His clean, crisp scent filled her nose and his joyful eyes filled her sight. His hands still rested at her waist, the papers in one of them rattled in the breeze, her hands on his shoulders, and she froze, afraid that any movement would make him let go and step away. And she did not want him to let go. Did she? Her body gave a resounding "no," but her mind flew to the multitude of reasons why she should. She stepped back and dropped her arms to her sides awkwardly. "That's great! So, so great!" Her vocabulary had taken the midnight train to Georgia, or something.

"Yeah," his voice rose in pitch a little and he cleared his throat. "She...uh...she said I can borrow some tools and a tool belt until I have money to buy my own. But I need some steel-toed boots. Do you think the shelter would have any?"

"That's great." Kaylee winced inside at her third use of "that's great" in the last ten seconds. "I mean, that's really nice of her. Let's go see if the shelter has boots."

Blayne's face turned sullen, and he looked at the ground and mumbled. "Did you get a hold of my parents?"

"Oh," Kaylee clapped her hands together, "yes! I talked to your mom, and she was so sweet and so relieved to know you're okay. She cried the whole time—happy tears. She's going to overnight your birth certificate to my parents' house then my mom will overnight it here."

He nodded. "So, she doesn't have my Social Security Card? It must have been in my wallet that got stolen my second night on the streets." Although he didn't comment on her description of his mom's reaction, the hurt and hope mixed in his eyes told her he cared.

"She said she thought you had taken it with you."

"Are we going to be able to get one with just my birth certificate?"

For no reason other than her skin itched to touch him again, she laid her hand on his arm. "That depends. Does your new job supply you an employee I.D.? With a picture?"

His head jerked up, and he beamed at her, the dimple in his left cheek teasing her. "Yes! In fact, we did that today so I can get onto the site in the morning." He pulled a laminated I.D. with a metal clip out of his pocket and showed it to her.

She squeezed his arm and smiled back at him. "Will you need a ride in the morning?"

His smile faded. "You've done so much for me already. Maybe for this first day, it would be a good idea to get a ride, just so I can time the walk back to the encampment. I don't want to be late." He looked at her and bit at his bottom lip, shaking his head. "And, I have one more favor to ask."

Kaylee nodded encouragement.

"Can we go somewhere where I can charge my media player after we find some boots? I'm going to need to use it as an alarm clock."

"No problem. Besides, this calls for a celebration, anyway. My treat—as long as we go cheap." She remembered their conversation about her finances and winced. "The McDonald's over by the college has chargers at some of the tables."

"Okay," he looked down at the employee badge in his hand. "But this is the last time you treat. Next time we eat together—I'm buying." He reached up and pushed a stray lock of hair out of her face, his fingers leaving tendrils of prickling heat on her skin where they brushed against it.

"It's a deal."

CHAPTER 13

Blayne worked through the New Year holiday, excited to be getting holiday pay for New Year's Day. He'd refused to let her drive him to or from work after the first day and it had been a few days since she'd seen him. Kaylee threw on some sweats and hurried down to the apartment's mail slot—his birth certificate should be there today.

She inserted her key into the slot and released the breath she'd been holding—it was there. She couldn't even fool herself into thinking she was excited because it meant Blayne could get his Social Security Card. It was really because that meant she would get to see him.

Since his boss had told him she'd give him a little time to go get his card replaced as soon as the birth certificate got there, Kaylee hurried to get ready and headed to the work site on campus. Having no idea how to find him, she parked next to the construction trailer, got out, and knocked on the door.

"Can I help you?" A woman wearing a hardhat, brown hair with gray streaks hanging to just past her chin beneath it, answered the door.

"Um, yes. My name is Kaylee."

The woman smiled. "Ahh. You're Blayne's *friend*. He said you might be stopping by within the next day or two. My name is Kelly." She reached out, and they shook hands. She had a strong grip. "I'll go get him, I wouldn't want your pretty hair to get messed up wearing one of these." She tapped on her hardhat. "I haven't had a good hair day in twenty years."

Kaylee laughed as Kelly stepped out of the trailer. She laughed again as she heard her yell, "Hey, new guy! You have a visitor!"

Blayne skipped most of the stairs as he rushed into the trailer. His nose was red from the cold and a few days' worth of stubble gave him a rugged, handsome look. He pulled his hardhat off and smiled. "Hi."

"Hi," Kaylee replied. "Your birth certificate came today."

"That's what I figured."

Kelly stood behind him in the open door. "Take an early lunch and go get your Social Security Card so I can pay you on Friday."

Blayne turned to her. "Thank you, Kelly. I'll be back as soon as I can."

"I don't expect it to be too soon," she said. "It's January second which means the Social Security office will probably be packed."

"Well," Blayne looked down. "I really appreciate you giving me time to go. I know we're running behind here."

"Not as far behind as we were before you came along. You're a hard worker and I appreciate that."

The back of his neck flushed pink. "Thank you. And thank you for giving me a chance."

"See you when you get back." Kelly stepped away from the door so they could leave.

Blayne set his hardhat and tool belt in Kaylee's back seat before sitting himself in the passenger seat.

"Sounds like things are going well." Kaylee buckled her seatbelt and waited for Blayne to do the same before starting the car.

"Yes. Kelly is enthusiastic about me learning how to do new things on the site. It's been invigorating to work hard."

"I'm so glad it worked out." She reached into the backseat and grabbed some papers to hand him. "I printed these off the internet. I thought you could start filling them out while we drive. Hopefully it'll save us some time when we get there."

It didn't end up saving much time, they still had to wait in a long line. But once they got to the front, it didn't take long at all. The man at the window took Blayne's papers, his birth certificate, and his work

I.D., typed it all into the computer, and said, "The actual card will be mailed to you and should arrive within ten business days. Do you need me to print off a temporary card for you?"

"Yes, please." Blayne smiled down at Kaylee.

Back in the car, she asked, "Do you want to get a quick bite to eat before you go back to work?"

He frowned. "I promised you I'd pay next time, but I don't get paid until Friday."

"Well, I think we can negotiate something. How about I pay today, and you pay the next two times?"

His stomach growled, and they both laughed. "It's a deal. But let's go somewhere cheap and fast."

"Taco Bell it is."

AFTER DROPPING Blayne off at work, Kaylee headed to a post office so she could mail his birth certificate back to his mom as she'd promised. As she stepped out onto the stairs of the post office, she noticed a familiar figure leaving the bank next door. Mama C. Kaylee stood still and watched as the elderly woman dropped some papers into the garbage can just outside the bank. Kaylee moved when Mama C disappeared around the corner. She wandered over to the trash can, looked around to see if anyone was watching, then reached in and grabbed the papers laying on top of the other garbage.

"Claire Watson," she whispered as she read the name on the first paper, a check stub with the letters NYSTRS strewn across the top. The other paper, smaller and thicker than the first, said "United States Treasury" on it. *This one must be a social security check,* Kaylee thought, *but what's the first one?* She folded them, put them in her coat pocket, and hurried to her car.

Kaylee didn't even bother taking her coat off after she rushed into her apartment. She flipped her laptop open and searched "NYSTRS." *New York State Teacher's Retirement System.* Mama C had been a teacher. In New York. Such a long ways away from Denver.

She typed "Claire Watson" and "teacher" and "New York" into the search engine. A New York Post headline from ten years prior popped up: EARLY MORNING APARTMENT FIRE KILLS TWO. Her hand shook as she clicked on the article. She read:

A fire that swept through an apartment in northern Manhattan early Wednesday, killed two tenants, Daniel Watson age 58 and his son, Eugene Watson age 18. The two lived together, along with wife and mother, Claire Watson, in the ground-floor apartment where the fire started accidentally, most probably caused by a faulty power cord. Mrs. Watson was not in the apartment at the time of the fire.

The two-alarm fire started around 6:00 a.m. and quickly swept through the ground-floor apartment. Both victims' bodies were found by firefighters huddled together in a corner of the small bathroom.

The building had no fire alarm, a Fire Department official stated. "It is a very old building. By code it would not be required to."

Kaylee couldn't read anymore. Her eyes blurred from the tears she didn't even try to slow down. "Poor Mama C. No wonder she doesn't want to talk about her past," she whispered. She needed to find out more. Why hadn't Mama C been there? Were these two her only family? What about friends? She wiped her eyes and turned to the article again, skimming until she saw what she wanted to know.

Mrs. Watson, a school teacher at Westbrook High School in Manhattan, had left at her usual time of 5:30 a.m. to catch the subway to the other side of town. She could not be reached for comment.

Westbrook High School, Kaylee thought. It had been ten years—

there should still be some people there that would remember Mama C. She looked up the high school and punched the number into her phone. As she held it up to her ear, listening to it ring, she wondered, *what am I doing?* Before she could answer her own question, a bored female voice answered, "Westbrook High."

"Umm..." What was she going to say? She considered hanging up, but shook her head.

"Can I help you?" the voice said.

"Umm, yeah, yes." Kaylee squeezed her eyes shut and pinched the bridge of her nose. "Yes, sorry. I'm looking for someone who may have known a teacher that worked there ten years ago or longer."

"And what is the reason you are seeking this information?"

Crap. She should have thought this through before calling. *Truth or lie?* Truth. Mostly. She was sure Mama C didn't want anyone from her past knowing where she was, so she just wouldn't mention Denver. "I'm a psychology student and I'm doing my thesis about different ways people handle tragedy. I just need some information about a fire that happened about ten years ago."

"And..." Suspicion crept into her voice. "This teacher's name is?"

"Mama...I mean, Claire. Claire Watson."

"I knew Mrs. Watson, but you'll never be able to find her by talking to anyone here. Her friends have been trying to track her down for a decade. Either she's dead, or she doesn't want to be found."

Kaylee swallowed. "That's unfortunate. But I'd still like to talk to some of her past coworkers. Get a feel for what she was like before and after the, uh, fire."

"I don't think you're going to get anyone to talk to you. Mrs. Watson was a private woman before and a recluse after. Her friends will want to protect her privacy."

Yep, that was the Mama C she knew. "Well, could you maybe just ask around? And if anyone consents to talk to me, they can call me?"

"Okay, but I'm telling you the chances are slim to none. What's your number?" The woman sighed.

Kaylee recited her phone number, then ended the call. She'd give them a couple of days to call back, but if that didn't happen, she needed another plan. It had suddenly become of utmost importance for her to find out more about Mama C's past.

Now she needed to decide what to tell Blayne, if anything, about what she'd found out. She was most definitely not going to mention anything to Mama C. That would be a terrible idea.

CHAPTER 14

The winter sun had nearly set by the time Kaylee saw the dark form of Blayne leaving the construction site. He wasn't expecting her, but ever since she'd decided to tell him everything she'd found out about Mama C, she'd been as antsy as the new kid on the first day of school. She didn't want to lie to him. And he cared deeply about Mama C.

She stepped out of her car and yelled, "Blayne!" waving so he'd see her when he turned around.

Even in the darkness of twilight, she could see the smile blossom on his face. As he reached her, he said, "Wow. Twice in one day. It feels like my birthday."

She rolled her eyes and smiled back at him. "I just thought maybe we could go for a ride."

His eyebrow rose up and his smile faltered. "A ride? Just out of the blue?"

"Yes." She tilted her head. "A ride. There's something I want to talk to you about."

"Uh oh. That sounds ominous. If we were dating, I'd think this was The Breakup."

A nervous laugh flew from her lips. "Nothing ominous. I promise." At least she hoped he wouldn't see her snooping as a bad thing. Now her smile faltered. Would he? There was no turning back.

"Okay then. Let's go for a ride." He turned toward the passenger side of her car, but stopped mid-stride. "Or, to save your gas, would you like to go for a walk instead?"

"Aren't you tired after working all day?"

"Not too tired to go for a walk with you. And you can show me the highlights of this campus, since I never leave the construction site when I'm here."

"Okay, let me grab my scarf and gloves. We can walk along Cherry Creek." She bent into her car to grab the items from the middle console.

Cherry Creek was close by the business building. They walked slowly and in silence for several minutes.

"Well," Blayne broke the silence, "what non-ominous news do you have to tell me?"

How should she start?

She had no idea, so she just plunged in. "I saw Mama C today when I went back downtown to mail your birth certificate back."

"Oh?" He raised an eyebrow.

She swallowed. "Um, yeah. She was leaving a bank right next to the post office I was at." *Keep going,* she thought. "She threw some papers away and I...I..." Kaylee huffed out a breath and raised her hands in surrender. "I snooped."

"You dug through the trash?" His eyebrow raised even higher, nearly touching his hairline.

Kaylee looked down. "I'm not proud of it, but, yes."

"Do I even want to know what you found out?" There was both a touch of curiosity and a touch of irritation in his voice.

"I don't know. *Do* you?"

Halting, Blayne reached for her arm to stop her beside him. He turned to her. "You know how private a person Mama C is. I know you're curious about her past, so am I. But I don't want to break her trust—she's the only reason I'm still alive." His forehead knotted and his eyes narrowed as if he'd just had a thought that angered him. "Is this personal information going to make it into your *thesis*? Is that all you care about here? No thought for her wishes, college girl?"

Kaylee shook her head so hard her ponytail slapped her in the face. "No. I'm only using the information she willingly gave me for that. I already have that part of it written up." Blayne didn't relax his face. Kaylee grew frustrated that he didn't believe her. "I mean it, Blayne! I just want to help her."

"And, will this new information 'help her'?"

"I think it can. That's why I wanted to tell you, to see what your opinion is."

Finally, his face softened somewhat. "Okay, tell me then."

She took a breath to shake off her frustration. "She threw away two check stubs—one that I'm pretty sure is Social Security, the other from a New York teacher's retirement fund."

"Okay, you found out where her money is coming from. How will this help her?" His expression and voice stayed neutral.

She couldn't help but let a little excitement show. "I found out more than that. She's getting older, Blayne. I'm worried about her health out on the streets. What if she has some family somewhere who would take her in? I bet she has access to health insurance from Medicare and maybe even through her teacher's retirement—that's something she can fall back on if...if her health demands she get out of the elements."

Concern laced his voice. "What do you know about her health? Do you think she's sick?"

"I don't know for sure. She has been coughing a lot lately and I'm worried about her. She just brushes me off when I say something."

He nodded and ran a hand through his hair, gazing down at the stream, the edges trimmed with a thin layer of ice. "I've noticed that, too." He swallowed a couple of times. "What else did you find out?"

Glad they were on the same page, Kaylee felt better about spilling the rest. "Once I knew her full name, and that she came from New York City and used to be a teacher, I did an internet search with those three things." She cleared her throat, trying to rid it of the emotion building up there. Her voice didn't respond, coming out all wavery, tears forming in the corners of her eyes. "She...there was a fire. She was on her way to work and her apartment caught on fire." She reached out and gripped Blayne's hand, needing human contact.

"Her husband and only child, a son, were killed in the fire." Losing all control, she dropped his hand and turned away from him, a sob rocking her chest.

She wiped at her eyes, afraid to turn around. It had been several seconds and Blayne hadn't uttered a sound. His steel-toed boots clomped as he stepped closer. Kaylee flinched when he laid his hands on her shoulders. Without thinking, she leaned back against him, needing the comfort the closeness would bring. His strong arms enveloped her in a hug from behind, his arms crossing just below her neck. He laid his head on top of hers and they stood that way for several minutes. Kaylee gained control over her emotions but didn't want to move. Her heart pounded in her chest, but rarely had anything felt so good—or so right—before.

The sun had fallen beyond the horizon and the wind picked up. The sliver of a moon and cloud-covered stars gave off little light. If not for the lights spread around the campus, it would have been pitch black out. She shivered from the chill.

With one last squeeze, he let go of her and stepped back. "We should get going before you freeze."

She crossed her arms, trying to hold in some warmth, and turned around to face him, nodding. "Let me give you a ride. I'd like to check in on Mama C, anyway."

"Okay. And we can talk more on the way."

In the car she turned the heat up full blast and Blayne got right to the talking. "I don't think we should say anything to Mama about this."

"I agree. Mostly because I'm afraid she'd throw both of us to the curb if we did." Kaylee pulled out onto the deserted street.

"And she won't let us help her for sure if she knows we've—you've—been snooping around, breaking promises, again. Speaking of snooping"—he narrowed his eyes—"how exactly do you intend to find out if she has any other family or close friends?"

Her stomach flipped at the hidden venom in the word *again*. She rushed to answer his question, determined not to hide anything from him. Determined to regain his trust. "I already called the school she used to teach at. The secretary said she remembers her and that she still has friends teaching at the school, but she wouldn't answer any of my other questions. Do you have any suggestions?"

"Yeah. Leave it alone, maybe." He shook his head. "She doesn't want any of this." He stared out the passenger window. "I thought you were past that."

Kaylee frowned. She'd been starting to think he was on her side here. He was right, though. She had dug where Mama C had forbidden her to dig. And it wasn't just Mama C's trust she'd stepped on but Blayne's too. Heck, would she even be able to keep her promise not to mention any of this to Mama?

But she had to pursue answers, didn't she? For Mama C? Her brain switched gears, going into overdrive—people were more likely to answer questions in person. She could use her credit card, or maybe her dad would let her use some of his airline points.

"What are you thinking, Kaylee?"

Sometimes he was too perceptive. She swallowed. Best to just spit it out. "Just about ways I might get to New York."

"Oh, no. Have you ever been to New York? No way you should go there by yourself. That place is waiting for a girl like you to step foot there. Your innocent face practically screams 'mug me'!" He shuddered and added in a quieter tone, "Or worse."

She pulled to her usual parking spot a couple dozen yards from the viaduct. "Don't worry. There's almost no way I can afford a trip there, anyway."

"Almost?" The corners of his mouth turned down.

Kaylee shook her head. "I mean, I *could* use my credit card."

Blayne whipped his head around, mouth open.

"But, I won't," she spoke before he could, "because that's crazy. Right?"

"Right. Crazy and stupid. And I know you're neither."

"Right. I'm not crazy or stupid." *But a smart person would figure out how to get it done.*

"Kaylee..."

She unbuckled her seatbelt and put the keys in her coat pocket. "Let's go see how Mama C is doing." She got out of the car before he could say anything else.

He shut his door a little harder than necessary. Kaylee concentrated on walking toward the small fire where she could see the outlines of several people. Blayne caught up to her, but didn't say anything.

Mama C sat near the fire, wrapped up in her sleeping bag. "Kaylee, come sit by me and get warm." She spread part of her sleeping bag out for Kaylee to sit on.

"Thank you, Mama C. How are you feeling tonight?"

"Same as the last time you asked." In straight up contrast to her reply, she broke out into a fit of coughing, holding a hand tight to her chest.

Kaylee raised an eyebrow at her.

"Now, young lady, don't go looking at me like that." A couple more coughs. "It's just a little cough, nothing worse than the common cold."

Kaylee and Blayne exchanged looks from where he stood on the other side of the faltering flame. "Okay. I won't argue with you," Kaylee said. "Have you eaten anything tonight? Are you drinking plenty of water?"

"She hasn't ate nothing," Hannah said. "I offered to make her a sandwich, but she said no."

Kaylee pushed herself up. "How about something warm, Mama? Do you have anything like that over here?" She walked over to where a new pile of grocery bags lay, tucked up against a cement column.

"No sense in looking," Mama C said. "I bought some chicken noodle soup, but someone stole our only pan."

"Well," Kaylee put her hands on her hips, "you need to eat. I'll be right back." She hurried to her car before anyone could try to stop her. She drove to the nearest Super-store and bought a cheap pan and some cough drops. Then she went to a drive-thru and ordered a

Styrofoam bowl of chicken noodle soup and a bottle of water. As she pulled up to the window, she decided to get the others something too, she knew Blayne hadn't eaten anything yet. She ordered from the "cheap" menu and set the bulging bag of chicken sandwiches and fries on the passenger seat and balanced the soup on the console next to her.

Blayne paced back and forth near where she usually parked, and he hurried to open her door as soon as the car stopped. "She had another coughing fit, worse this time."

Kaylee shook her head, worry piercing her heart. "Help me carry this stuff, please." She handed him the bag of food and she grabbed the bag with the pan and cough drops and the container of soup.

"You need to stop doing this," Blayne said.

"What?" Kaylee put on an innocent act.

"Spending money on us."

She stopped and turned to him. "Look, it's my money and—just like Mama C—I'll do what I want with it." She smiled to soften her tone.

Under his breath, Blayne whispered, "Until you run out."

She rolled her eyes and continued on to where Mama C sat. Gravel dug into her knees as she knelt beside the elderly woman. She sat the bag next to her. "Here's a new pan and some cough drops." Kaylee peeled the top off the steaming soup, plopped a plastic spoon in it, and handed it to Mama C. "Please eat the whole thing. It's the best soup in Denver." She screwed the top off the water bottle then screwed it back on loosely. "Here's some water to go with it."

"You are the sweetest." Mama C slurped a bite of soup, closed her eyes, and hummed, "Mmm mmm."

Blayne handed out the warm sandwiches and fries, taking two sandwiches for himself. "You really are the sweetest," he whispered as he sat down next to her. Some of the tension still present from their earlier discussion eased from Kaylee's shoulders.

CHAPTER 15

The apartment was a mess. Allie had spent all of her time at Max's before he had to leave on his next away rotation in Arizona. Kaylee had spent all her time upholding her promise to Mama C to help Blayne. She sighed as she surveyed the dishes piled high in the sink, the takeout packages littering the countertop, and the dust built up on the coffee table. She opened the fridge. A half-gallon of expired milk and some condiments. "Cleaning tonight, shopping tomorrow," she said to herself.

She changed into her "sloppy clothes," pajama bottoms and a Captain America t-shirt, and started in on the kitchen. As she cleaned, she let her mind run wild. By the time she'd completed the dusting and ran a vacuum over the small area of carpet, she'd decided she needed to go to New York. It was more important than worry about racking up more debt. As her head hit the pillow well after her usual bedtime, she decided she'd work the "dad" angle first.

Using the "I need to do this for my thesis project" angle, Kaylee was able to convince her dad to use some of his credit card points to buy her airline ticket. She only felt slightly guilty about the partial lie—it was *because of* her thesis that she'd stumbled onto this mystery.

She booked her flight for the middle of the next week and used her credit card to reserve a room at the cheapest hotel she could find. She'd have to use a ride-share company to get around, from what she'd researched about the subway system, it would be much too confusing for her to figure out.

And she needed to break the news to Blayne. He was not going to be happy, but she didn't want to lie to him.

After she made the arrangements for New York, Kaylee finished cleaning up the apartment. By the time Allie rolled out of bed near noon, Kaylee's stomach reminded her she hadn't eaten since sometime the day before. She stepped in front of her sleepy roommate. "Get dressed. Let's go to lunch and then get a few groceries."

Allie drew her eyebrows together and pointed to her ear. "I can't hear you," she growled.

"Ha ha. Very funny." Kaylee rolled her eyes. "*I know you aren't a morning person, but it's no longer morning,*" she signed, then pointed to the clock on the microwave.

"Ugh. Fine. As long as lunch includes copious amounts of coffee." Allie pivoted and stomped back into their shared room.

They went to their favorite diner for breakfast where Kaylee told Allie her plans for New York the next week.

"You can't be serious." Allie raised her voice to the point where the neighboring tables turned to look at them.

"*Lower your voice,*" Kaylee signed.

"*Sorry,*" she signed back and then spoke in a slightly muted voice, "but, this is crazy. You can't go to NYC by yourself."

"I'll be fine. I'm only going to the school. I promise to be back in my hotel room before dark. I'll really only be there for one full day, I'm flying in on Tuesday, visiting the school on Wednesday, and flying home on Thursday."

"Maybe I should go with you. How much are plane tickets?"

"A lot. I was only able to swing it because I'm using my dad's points."

Allie took a sip of her coffee. "Well, I'm still going to look at flights."

LATER THAT EVENING, at a time she was sure Blayne would be there after work, Kaylee went to check on Mama C.

She didn't see his tall frame among those gathered around the fire, but before she could be too disappointed, Demarcus hurried over to her. "Mama C has a fever. You don't happen to have some medicine for that, do you?"

"Actually," Kaylee raised her left arm that had a bag looped around it, "I do. And some fresh water and more soup."

Demarcus smiled, but it wasn't his usual carefree smile, his eyes continued to show worry even as his lips curled up at the ends. "You're the best."

Kaylee knelt down next to Mama C and felt her forehead. She was burning up. Kaylee opened the large bottle of water she pulled from the bag and handed it to her. Mama C took a small drink and then suffered a bout of coughing that shook her thin frame.

Popping two cold and flu pills out of a blister pack, Kaylee handed them to the elderly woman. "Here. These will help with your cough and fever. I hope."

Mama C worked on swallowing the pills while Kaylee removed the top from the steaming soup and plopped a plastic spoon in it. She traded Mama C for the water bottle, put the lid back on, and set it on the ground between them.

Kaylee stood and grabbed a couple of rolled up sleeping bags to prop up Mama C while she ate.

"Here, let me help." Blayne crouched down on the other side of Mama C and helped secure the sleeping bags. "How are you feeling today, Mama?"

"No worse than yesterday. You all need to quit fussing over me."

Blayne looked at Kaylee and raised his eyebrows.

"She has a fever today. I just gave her some medicine so it should come down within thirty minutes or so," Kaylee said in answer to his silent question.

"You all settled for a minute?" he asked Mama C.

"Yes. I'm fine. I'm just going to sit right here and finish eating this delicious soup Miss Kaylee brought me."

"Okay." Blayne patted her gently on the shoulder, then looked at Kaylee and jerked his head to the side. "Can I talk to you for a minute?"

Nodding, Kaylee stood and followed him, wondering if now would be a good time to tell him about New York.

When they stopped and faced each other, Kaylee looked up at him, waiting for him to speak. After a few awkward moments in which he looked from her to the ground several times, he said, "I get paid tomorrow."

"That's great!"

"It won't be a full check, because I only worked part of last week."

Kaylee nodded, not knowing what to say.

Blayne cleared his throat and looked her straight in the eyes. "I'd like to take you to dinner tomorrow. My treat, but you'll have to do the 'taking' part, since you're the one with the car."

She didn't want him to use his hard-earned money to take her to dinner, but she knew she needed to give him this one. And, she'd promised to let him buy the next meal they shared. The next *two* meals if she recalled correctly. "I'd love to. Do you want me to meet you here or at the job site?"

He smiled and answered quickly, "Meet me here around six. That way we can check on Mama before we go."

"It's a date," she said, her face instantly flushing with warmth. "Um, I mean..."

"Yes," he interrupted. "It is."

Now that their apartment was clean and somewhat stocked with groceries, Allie decided to invite Max over for dinner and a movie.

Kaylee had nothing else to do, so she joined them at Allie's insistence, feeling like a third-wheel.

"So," Allie said as soon as they all sat at the table to eat the "gourmet" spaghetti and garlic bread she'd cooked, "guess who has a date tomorrow?"

Max plastered a fake look of shock on his face, eyes and mouth open wide, and looked at Kaylee. "You? Like, a *real* date?"

Kaylee rolled her eyes at him and glared at her friend.

"Who's the lucky guy?" Max asked.

"Who do you think?" Allie said. "The only guy she's spent any time with for the last month."

Max tilted his head to the side. "The homele...I mean, Blayne? Really?"

Now was a good time for Kaylee to put a stop to this. "Yes. Blayne. He gets his first paycheck tomorrow, and he wants to take me to dinner. I agreed. End of discussion."

Ignoring her last statement, Max asked, "Are you sure this is a good idea? I mean, he has quite a *history*, you know."

"I know his history much better than you do," Kaylee snapped. "And it's just dinner. We've eaten together multiple times, and he's yet to murder me with a spork."

"I think it's uber-romantic," Allie said, stopping her boyfriend from saying whatever he'd been planning on saying next. "And you've met Blayne. He's a teddy bear."

"Some teddy bears have hidden teeth and claws," he mumbled.

"Oh my gosh! I'll be fine. I trust him." Kaylee stabbed a meatball with more gusto than necessary. "Now, change the subject."

And she did trust him. But did she deserve his trust? She would tell him about New York tonight. No more keeping things from him.

CHAPTER 16

Casual. That was the look Kaylee was going for. She wanted the "this is no big deal, just two friends having dinner" look with a splash of sexy...maybe a drop...a small drop. She settled for her favorite jeans, a tight sweater, and lip gloss.

Kaylee pulled up to the viaduct a little before six, checked her face in the sun-visor mirror, and stepped out into the cold, chastising herself for being so nervous. It was ridiculous, really. She'd eaten with Blayne on multiple occasions. She took a deep breath and focused in on Mama C as she stepped toward the camp.

"Mama C, how are you feeling tonight?" Kaylee knelt next to her and felt her forehead. Still a little warm, but not as fiery hot as the night before.

"Much better. Thank you, dear. Blayne had me take some more of that cold medicine and it's been keeping my fever down."

"How about the cough? Is it getting any better?"

"No," Blayne answered for her, stepping into the ring of firelight. "She nearly coughed herself into throwing up while she was eating a while ago."

"I'll see if Max can suggest anything else for her."

"Stop talking like I'm not here," Mama C said. "It's just a little cold. I'll be fine. Now, don't you two have plans? Get going. Hannah and Clint can babysit me tonight."

"Yep," Clint said. "We've got this." He sat next to Mama and handed her a water bottle.

"Okay, okay," Blayne said. "We're going."

"We won't wait up," Hannah said with a wink.

Kaylee looked at Blayne as the familiar warmth of embarrassment spread up her neck and into her face. He rolled his eyes and took her gently by the elbow, leading her toward her car.

"Ignore her," he said. "She loves to get a reaction out of people." He walked her to the driver's side and opened the door for her before going over to the passenger side to get in.

As he buckled his seatbelt, she asked, "Where to?"

"Well, like I said, this was only a partial paycheck. I was thinking somewhere cheap, like Danny's? Is that okay?"

"Danny's is perfect. I love their breakfasts." Kaylee turned the car around and headed for the street. She glanced over at him, noticing that he'd taken his beanie and gloves off. His hair was adorably messy. "You smell great." Crap. That wasn't what she'd meant to say. *Like, you usually stink, but tonight you smell okay,* she thought. *What a stupid thing to say.*

"Thank you," he didn't seem to mind her careless comment. "Kelly let me clean up in her trailer and Jorge spritzed me with cologne as I tried to escape."

"That was nice of them." Why was she being so awkward?

"Yeah. They're nice people." He turned in his seat to face her. "Thanks again for helping me get this job. It feels really good to be a productive member of society."

She smiled, feeling a little more at ease, yet still worried that it bothered him to have to depend on her for so much. "You're welcome." She pulled into the parking lot at Danny's and parked close to the entrance. She got out before Blayne had a chance to come around and open her door.

They were seated in a booth hidden from most of the other tables. Blayne slipped his coat off, folded it in half, and set it on the seat next to him.

"That's a nice shirt," Kaylee said as she slid across from him into the booth. "Is it new?"

He looked down at the blue, long-sleeve button-up. "Yeah. I, uh, stopped at Walmart to cash my check and they had these shirts on sale for practically nothing."

"The color really brings out your eyes." She refused to be embarrassed for telling him that, it was true, his blue eyes popped next to the color of his shirt.

"Well, thank you. You look great, too."

The waitress stopped at their table. "Hi, I'm Amy. Can I get you guys something to drink?"

"Water, please," Kaylee said. "With a slice of lemon."

"Same, but without the lemon," Blayne said.

Kaylee opened the menu to the breakfast page and searched for the best deals. "What are you going to have?"

"Probably a burger. If I recall, they have pretty good ones here," Blayne said. "What about you? Still sticking with the breakfast-for-dinner idea?"

"Yes. You can't go wrong with breakfast food."

"Or a hamburger."

"True."

The waitress reappeared. "One water with lemon," she set the glass in front of Kaylee, "and one without. Are you ready to order?"

Blayne nodded to Kaylee, so she went first. "I'll have the two-egg special, with bacon."

"How would you like your eggs?" Amy asked as she scribbled on her order pad.

"Over-easy," Kaylee said.

Amy looked at Blayne and smiled wide, cocking a hip out. "And, how about you?"

"A bacon cheeseburger," he glanced at Kaylee then back at the waitress. "No onions."

"You got it. I'll bring that right out as soon as it's done." Amy turned and sashayed away from their table.

They sat in uncomfortable silence for a few minutes. Blayne looked at the table tent for far too long, and Kaylee looked around at the wall decorations.

"I have an idea." Kaylee broke the silence. "Let's ask each other questions to get to know each other better." Blayne held up a hand and opened his mouth, but Kaylee hurried to finish before he could speak. "If I ask something you don't want to answer, just say 'pass.'"

"Okay," he said slowly. "You ask first."

She crooked her mouth into a mischievous smile. "Do you have any tattoos?"

"Nope. I could never afford one and now I don't want one." Blayne matched her smile. "Do you have any?"

Kaylee swallowed, trying to keep the embarrassment at bay. "It... it was my one act of rebellion against my parents' wishes—when I turned eighteen. They still don't know I have it."

Blayne's eyebrows rose. "Where is it? And what is it?"

"That's two questions, but I'll let it pass. It's on my side," she pointed to the right side of her torso, "and it's...well, I'm a little obsessed with Harry Potter, so it's a symbol from that."

"The Deathly Hallows?" Blayne asked, surprising her.

"You know Harry Potter?"

"Of course I do. I read all seven books when I was in elementary school. I watched the movies over and over up until I left home."

"The books are better," they both said at the same time, then laughed.

"What's your favorite book in the series?" Kaylee asked.

"That's a tough question, but I think it's probably The Prisoner of Azkaban. I love the whole Sirius angle. What's your favorite?"

"Prisoner is second on my list. My favorite is The Goblet of Fire. That's when things start to get real, in the graveyard, when Cedric dies."

"Yeah. That's a good one."

"I could talk about Harry Potter all night, so I'm going to move on to the next question so that doesn't happen," Kaylee said. "What's your favorite color?"

"It changes day to day. Today,"—he stared into her eyes—"it's golden brown, like fresh honey glinting in the sun."

Kaylee's eye color was strange and nobody had been able to pinpoint it before. Blayne had described it perfectly.

He continued, still looking in her eyes, his voice sounding silky. "What's your favorite color?"

Kaylee tried to tear her eyes away from his but couldn't. Words stumbled out of her mouth in awkward waves. "It's always been the same." *He's going to think I'm copying him,* she worried. "...since I was little, my room was..." Her eyes still locked with his. "Blue. My favorite color is blue."

Blayne's mouth twitched. He reached toward her face. His fingers barely brushed her cheek, when the waitress interrupted. He pulled his hand away and turned to face her.

"Be careful," Amy said, "the plates are hot."

The spell broken, they looked at Amy and both said, "Thank you." Kaylee spread her napkin on her lap and started mushing up her eggs, adding salt and pepper.

Blayne slathered his burger with ketchup and took a big bite.

Kaylee took a small bite of eggs and, after swallowing, asked, "Who's your favorite female singer?" continuing their getting-to-know-you game.

He finished chewing and swallowed before answering. "Would you think less of me if I said it was Taylor Swift?"

"Um, Yes."

"Okay, good, because it isn't her. It's Pink." He tore off another bite of his burger and smiled, ketchup smeared on his top lip.

Nodding, Kaylee said, "Yeah. Pink's awesome."

As he wiped the ketchup from his mouth with the back of his hand, Kaylee couldn't help but be drawn to his lips, only realizing she was staring when they turned up into a roguish smile. She glanced at his eyes and quickly looked down at her plate when she recognized the glint of silent laughter.

"Tell me about your family," Blayne said.

Thankful he didn't comment on the magnetic draw his lips had held her in a moment ago, she answered, "It's just my mom and dad and me and my brother. My brother's fifteen. He's a cool kid, really great running back. He plays on the varsity team already. My dad and I are really close and he is a big worry-wart. Before I left for college, he took me to the gun range a few times to teach me how to shoot. He wanted me to get a handgun, but I don't really want that responsibility."

Blayne nodded and shoved three fries into his mouth.

While he chewed, Kaylee asked, "What about your family? What are they like?" She knew she'd made a mistake when he stopped chewing and dropped his hand to the table. She didn't retract it, though. She'd told him at the start that he could say "pass" if he didn't want to answer anything.

He swallowed and glanced back up at Kaylee. "I pa... Oh, what the hell. My parents are great. They tried everything they could think of to help me. I have a little sister who's twelve years younger than me." His voice lowered and a look of anguish passed over his face. "She's why I left."

They ate in silence for several minutes, Kaylee worrying that she'd ruined the whole night. But she was also more curious than ever. What could have happened with his sister that made him think he had to leave home? She recalled one of their first conversations in which he'd said something about putting his sister in danger.

With counterfeit cheeriness infused in his voice, Blayne broke the silence. "Tell me about your favorite birthday."

Kaylee smiled. This was an easy one. "When I turned eleven. My grandma and my mom threw me the best birthday party ever. It started with me getting a letter from Hogwarts."

"That's awesome!" Blayne laughed. "A Harry Potter themed birthday."

"It was a blast." She thought back on the "potions class" where the potions were made from candy; the Quidditch game; the homemade Butterbeer. Her mom and grandma had gone all out. "Your turn," she said. "Your best birthday."

"I had a lot of great ones." He thought for a few seconds. "The best was probably when I got my dirt bike. I'd wanted one for so long. It was a blast."

He shoved the last fry in his mouth then put his napkin on top of his empty plate just as Kaylee took the last bite of her toast. "I get the last question," he said, "since you asked the first."

Uh oh, Kaylee thought, *there's that twinkle in his eyes again.* She held her breath, waiting for his question.

He leaned across the table and whispered, "Do you kiss on a first date?"

Her stomach flipped so hard and so fast she thought she'd lose all the food she just ate. She inhaled a little too sharply and sucked saliva into her lungs. Her face, already red from embarrassment—or maybe excitement—turned a whole new shade of crimson as she coughed for two minutes solid.

Concern on his face, Blayne handed her some water. "You okay?"

She nodded, still unable to speak. She took a couple of sips of water and cleared her throat. "I'm fine." Her words came out raspy. She hoped she hadn't done permanent damage to her vocal cords.

"Good," he smiled, "then you can answer my question now."

Okay, she thought. *Time to show some daring. You know there was a reason you couldn't take your eyes off his lips.* Kaylee cleared her throat again. In her still raspy voice, she said, "I haven't in the past." She looked him straight in the deep blue eyes. "But sometimes, rules are meant to be broken."

Blayne sat back, his smile turning from one of mischief to one of anticipation.

"Will this be separate checks?" Amy-of-the-bad-timing asked.

"No," Blayne said, not taking his eyes from Kaylee. "Just one."

A small pout pursed Amy's lips as she ripped the ticket from her pad and pushed it toward Blayne on the table. "You can pay at the counter. Have a great evening." She trounced away.

Grabbing the bill, Blayne scooted out of the booth and held a hand out to help Kaylee up. "What do you want to do now?"

Kaylee could hardly think straight at the moment—Blayne hadn't let go of her hand after he'd helped her stand, and warm tingles raced up her arm straight into her chest. Plus, she was still thinking about that last question he'd asked. "Umm..." Her thoughts flashed to Mama C and her cough. "Let's go to Max's and see if he has any suggestions for Mama C."

KAYLEE PARKED NEXT to Max's car, turned the ignition off, and with a shy smile, glanced at Blayne before opening her door to get out. Before she'd even turned to shut her door, Blayne was standing next to her. He put a hand on her arm. "Wait just a minute. I have a favor to ask you."

Turning to fully face him, she nodded, looking up into his eyes.

He swallowed and licked his lips. "Will you keep my money for me?" He rushed to explain. "I can't get a bank account without an address, plus living on the streets is a good way to get everything you own stolen." Another lick of his lips. "And I'd like to save up for a place to live—just a room or studio apartment—now that I have a job."

A smile spread wide across her face and she held herself back from throwing her arms around him. He was really doing it! He was really getting his life together! "Of course, I will. And I'll help you look for a place."

He took her shoulders in his hands and stepped closer to her, staring down into her face with a smile. "Thank you." His gaze shifted from her eyes to her lips and back. His smile faded and his tongue darted out to lick his lips again nervously.

Kaylee's throat went dry and her heart pounded in her ears. Was this too soon? Should she pull away? Her muddled brain couldn't decide, but her lips knew what they wanted. She tilted her head up and wet her lips. Blayne's hands tightened on her shoulders and he pulled her closer, his mouth lowering...

"Hey, Kaylee!" Max called from his small deck. "What's up?"

The spell broken, Blayne dropped his hands and backed away. He stared at the ground and put his hands in his pockets.

"Uh, hi Max." Kaylee yelled. "We'll be up in a second." *He did that on purpose,* she thought. *He doesn't trust Blayne yet. Jerk.* With an apologetic smile she shrugged and boldly grabbed Blayne's hand with a defiant look up at Max and led him to the stairs leading up to Max's apartment.

Max held the door open for them, Allie stood behind him, her mouth tilted up in a knowing smirk. "Hey, Kay, Blayne! How was the date?"

Blayne looked down at Kaylee. "Hopefully not over yet."

Her stomach flipped, and she bit her bottom lip to keep her smile from taking over her entire face. She cleared her throat of the large stone-like lump that had formed there in the last two seconds. "It's been great,"—she flicked her gaze up at Blayne—"so far."

Motioning toward the couch, Max said, "Come in and have a seat. What brings you to visit?"

Kaylee sat first, leaving the choice to Blayne of how close to sit to each other. He left a couple of inches between them—just enough so their legs brushed against each other if one of them moved. Allie and Max sat in chairs across from them. Kaylee noted how Max had positioned the chairs at an angle to make it easier for Allie to turn and read his lips as they spoke.

"We have a medical question for you, Max," Kaylee said. "Mama C has been sick for several days now and seems to be getting worse."

"What kind of symptoms is she having?" Max leaned forward, in full almost-a-doctor mode at the mention of illness.

"Coughing mostly," Kaylee answered.

"And shortness of breath," Blayne added. "She was huffing so hard yesterday after a trip to the store, I thought she was going to pass out."

Max nodded. "Is she coughing anything up? Has she had a fever?"

"She's definitely had a fever," Kaylee said.

"And she sounds like she's hacking up a lung," Blayne wrinkled his nose, "but don't ask me what color the mucous is, that stuff makes me want to throw up."

Max laughed. "Yeah. That isn't my favorite thing either." He turned serious, a little V appearing between his eyes. "Sounds like she may have pneumonia. She should really go see a doctor."

"She won't," Kaylee and Blayne answered at the same time.

Allie, who had been turning from face to face as she followed their conversation, spoke up. "Max can go take a look at her. We aren't doing anything right now."

Kaylee perked up. "Would you, Max? That would be awesome. I've been giving her cold medicine and making her drink fluids and eat soup, but that's about the extent of my medical skills."

Max turned to Allie and raised an eyebrow. "Yeah, guess I can go do a quick exam on her." He stood and walked down the hall to his room, soon reappearing with a stethoscope around his neck.

Zipping up her coat, Allie smiled. "Let's go."

Max frowned and signed to her, *Why don't you stay here. I won't be long.*

Allie rolled her eyes. *Quit worrying. I'll be fine. Kaylee has been hanging out with these guys for weeks.*

"Come on you two," Kaylee said. "You know you aren't going to change her mind, Max."

With a sigh, Max pulled his jacket on and held the door open for the rest of them.

KAYLEE PARKED as close to the encampment as she could and left her headlights on at Max's insistence—so he "could see to examine Mama C."

Blayne approached the small group first, Mama C eyeing him with a deep frown. "You look nice, Blayne." She lowered her voice to a hoarse growl. "But why you bringing people..." She broke off into a rattling cough that wracked her small body in fitful spasms.

Worry creasing his face, Blayne knelt down next to her and supported her back as she hacked, Kaylee kneeling on her other side. The coughing ceased, Mama C leaned back against his arm, her chest heaving up and down with each ragged breath. It took several minutes for her lips to return to a pale pink from the blue color they'd turned.

"Mama," Blayne touched her forehead, "you're burning up, and that cough is getting worse. Kaylee's friend is a doctor, and he agreed to come and take a look at you."

"I don't need a doctor, Blayne. I told you to just let nature take its course."

Blayne shook his head. "Just let him listen to your lungs. Please."

"Fine." She reached to pat Kaylee's hand. "Tell your friend he can come listen." Her eyes flicked to where Max and Allie stood ten feet away and she chuckled. "And tell them I don't bite."

Kaylee motioned them over and moved out of the way so Max could get to Mama C.

"Hi, ma'am," Max said, squatting beside her. "I'm Max. Can I help you get your coat off so I can listen to your lungs?"

Mama C nodded and pushed the blankets and sleeping bag down onto her lap, then unzipped her coat. Max and Blayne helped her out of it. She clenched her jaw, shivering, but didn't say anything.

Max put the earpieces of his stethoscope in his ears and held the diaphragm to her back. "Take a deep breath in and out."

She got halfway through an inhale and broke into another long coughing spell. By the time Max had listened to all the lobes of her lungs, several minutes and several more coughing spells had passed.

Quietly, Max helped Mama C put her coat back on. Blayne pulled her blankets back up to her chin and helped her ease back down against the rolled up sleeping bag she'd been leaning against. They stood and Kaylee and Allie stepped closer to them.

"Well?" Kaylee asked.

Max shook his head. "She definitely has pneumonia in both lungs. I'm sure she isn't getting enough oxygen. She should really be in a hospital."

"That's not gonna' happen, young man," Mama C said.

"Why are you so stubborn?" Blayne asked, an angry scowl crossing his face.

"Just born that way." Her voice softened. "Honey, if the Lord wills it, I'll get better. And if he doesn't, well, then..."

Max looked from Blayne to Kaylee and back at Mama C. "Will you at least let me give you some antibiotics?"

"Yes," Blayne answered for her. "She will."

"Blayne—"

"Mama," his voice rose. "If I have to roll you over and bare your butt cheek so he can give you a shot of penicillin, so help me, I will!"

Mama's eyes widened and Kaylee hid a smile.

"That won't be necessary," Max said, holding his hands up placatingly. "I have some pills back at the house, if Kaylee can run us back home, I can get them for you."

Blayne narrowed his eyes at Mama. "And she *will* take them."

"Are you allergic to anything, ma'am?" Max asked.

Mama shook her head and closed her eyes, seemingly resolved to do as Blayne demanded.

"How BAD IS IT?" Blayne asked once they were back in the car.

"Pretty bad," Max answered. "If she'd started taking antibiotics earlier on in the process, she'd probably be better. But the infection has progressed to the point where she really needs IV antibiotics, fluids, oxygen..."

"Can't you force her to go to the hospital?" Allie asked.

Max shook his head. "She could just sign herself out AMA—against medical advice—unless she doesn't have power of attorney for herself."

"What's 'power of attorney'?" Blayne asked.

"It's when a person either signs over their right to make decisions for themselves to someone else—usually a family member—or a judge decides a person isn't capable of making their own decisions and assigns power of attorney to someone, again, usually a family member."

"She doesn't have any family." Blayne frowned. "At least not that I know of."

Max leaned forward, his hand on the back of Kaylee's seat. "Maybe you'll find some relatives when you go to New York next week."

Kaylee winced and quickly glanced at Blayne before returning her gaze to the road. His face froze mid-frown. He turned to her, and after a moment of angry silence, said, "You're going to New York?"

She glared at Max in the rearview mirror. "I was going to tell you —tonight." She rushed on, babbling, not wanting to give him a chance to speak just yet. "I didn't put it on my credit card, my dad let me use his points. It'll only be for a couple of days and I'll be really careful. I won't leave the hotel after dark, I won't ride the subway, I won't take my purse with me..."

"Stop," Blayne spat.

She chanced a look at him and immediately regretted it. His beautiful eyes held anger, hurt, and worry all wrapped up in a scowl she hadn't seen since their first couple of weeks of knowing each other.

Blayne whipped his head around, facing the passenger side window. "It's really none of my business, it seems."

They rode in silence to Max's apartment, Max and Allie signing to each other in the back seat. Blayne waited in the car while Kaylee followed them inside to get the medication.

"I'm sorry, Kaylee," Max said as they tromped up the stairs. "I thought you'd have told him by now."

Kaylee shrugged, not ready to forgive him just yet.

Once inside, Max went into his room to get the pills. Allie turned to her friend. "I'm sorry Max did that. Blayne looked furious."

"Yeah," Kaylee said. "He doesn't think I'll be safe there by myself." *And I still don't think he likes the idea of me digging into Mama C's past.*

"I'm a little worried about that myself. I looked into flights and I'm afraid they're out of my price range." Allie laid a hand on Kaylee's shoulder and squeezed.

Kaylee smiled slightly. "I'll be okay. It can't be that much worse than Denver, can it?"

Rattling a bottle of pills, Max stepped into the living room. "Here," he handed them to Kaylee, "she'll need to take one pill twice a day. I hope it's enough to help her turn the corner."

"Me, too." Kaylee put the bottle in her jacket pocket and thanked him. She hugged Allie. "See you at home."

Blayne continued to stare out the window as Kaylee pulled out into the street. Anxiety and anger fought inside her, making her stomach roll with nausea. It really was none of his business, it wasn't like she was his girlfriend or anything. Who was he to tell her what she should and shouldn't do? But on the other hand, she really liked him, and the thought of him being mad at her hurt, physically and emotionally. She pressed a hand to her chest, trying to calm the rising pressure there.

They both remained silent until they were almost to the viaduct. Blayne sighed and finally turned to look at her. "You're crazy, you know, going to New York by yourself."

She shrugged, relieved that he was speaking to her, but not quite trusting her voice yet.

"I don't want you to go," he continued, "but I understand that you feel you need to. I'm just really worried about you. I keep envisioning all the bad things that could happen to you." He looked out the windshield and ran his hand through his hair, clearing his throat. His voice came out quieter and a little raspy. "I can't stand it. Those thoughts. They're making me crazy and you haven't even left yet."

Kaylee stopped the car near the viaduct. She swallowed the lump that had formed in her throat at his words. All anger gone as she realized how much he cared about her despite all the half-truths and secrets she'd kept from him. Despite his feelings of shame for needing her help. Kaylee wanted to deserve his worry, wanted to be good enough and strong enough to be worthy of him. She reached for his hand and his fingers closed around hers in a tight grip. She whispered, "I'll be okay, Blayne. I promise."

He squeezed her hand, still staring out the front window. "I hope so."

CHAPTER 17

Over the next few days, Kaylee stopped to check on Mama C every day. Blayne was distant, only talking to her about Mama's condition. No sign that their thwarted first kiss was going to happen any time soon.

Mama seemed to be improving. Her fever broke on the second day of antibiotics, though her cough still worried Kaylee. She was eating and drinking better, but her stamina was still next to nothing. Blayne had kept some of the money from his paycheck, but had given the rest to Kaylee to keep safe for him. He'd used that money to buy more groceries for Mama and the kids.

Tuesday evening, Kaylee went to check on Mama one last time before her trip to New York the next day. After making sure she'd taken her medicine and eaten a good portion of her soup, Kaylee rose to leave.

"Kaylee," Blayne said. "Wait."

Her heart stuttered as he put his arm around her waist and led her off toward her car, stopping a few paces away. "I'm sorry," he looked down, "I know I haven't been fun to be around these last few days." He put his hands on her shoulders and looked her in the eyes.

The warmth from his hands spread through the fabric of her coat as his eyes burned into hers.

He swallowed. "I just don't want anything to happen to you." He looked up at the dark sky and exhaled, blowing a wisp of steam into the air. His voice shaking, he continued, "I really like you. And I want to see where this is going with us."

When he looked back down at her, his eyes glistened with unfallen tears. "I'm terrified that something will happen to you."

Kaylee had never seen his tough-guy exterior crack so drastically. Her heart ached. She threw herself against him and hugged him hard enough to crack a rib or two. "I'm going to be fine," she mumbled against his chest. "I'll be careful, I promise."

His arms enveloped her and he laid his cheek against the top of her head. They stood that way for several minutes, wrapped in each other's warmth as the cold wind swirled around them.

With a deep sigh, Blayne loosened his hold and leaned back to look into Kaylee's eyes. "I know I can't talk you out of going. Because you're as stubborn as a mule—or a drug addict." He smiled ruefully. "Kelly, my boss, gave me a cell phone yesterday. She said she needs to be able to get ahold of me, and the company will pay for it."

"That's great," Kaylee said. *For her and for me.*

"It is," Blayne agreed. "They've been really great to me." He cleared his throat and continued, "Kaylee, will you please text or call me when you get to your hotel? And when you leave your hotel. And when you get back to your hotel, and anytime day or night just so I know you're safe?"

Kaylee snort-laughed. Embarrassing. At least the embarrassment kept the threatening tears at bay. "How about this, I'll text you whenever I leave somewhere and get somewhere. And I'll call you when I'm in for the night."

Blayne released a held breath. "Deal."

She took his phone and entered her number into his contacts. "Text me so I have your number. You know I'm only going to be gone for a couple of days. I fly out tomorrow morning and I'll be back here early Friday evening."

"What time does your flight come in on Friday?"

"Four o'clock." She shivered as the breeze picked up and swept her hair into her face.

Moving the hair out of her face with a gentle touch, Blayne said, "I'll see you then. You'd better get going before you freeze." His gaze lingered on her lips for a second then he gave her a quick hug, walked her the rest of the way to her car, and opened the door for her.

As THE PLANE LANDED, Kaylee swallowed down a huge lump of anxiety that had taken up residence in her throat. She switched her phone off airplane mode and tapped a ride-share app as they taxied to the gate. Transportation taken care of from the airport to her hotel, Kaylee leaned back and closed her eyes, going over her plan again. Her thoughts quickly drifted to Blayne. She opened her eyes and sent a text to him.

Just landed.

Her phone buzzed as she exited the plane with her carry-on. She stepped to the side, out of the way of the other passengers as soon as she entered the terminal.

Blayne: *Good glad you made it there let me know when you get to the hotel*

Ugh, no punctuation, she thought with a smile.

Blayne: *Make sure the ride-share driver is really a ride-share driver check the license plate number*

Kaylee rolled her eyes. Now he sounded like her dad. She texted back, *Will do.*

She exited the airport and went to the pick-up spot, looking down at her phone. *Blue Prius. License plate # DWS 4376.*

A blue Prius pulled up to the sidewalk several cars down. Kaylee wandered in that direction, looking for the ride-share sticker in the window. The license plate number matched. She smiled and waved at the driver. He rolled the window down. "Kaylee?"

"Yes."

"Here," he opened his door, "let me get your stuff. Go ahead and get in."

The hour drive was pleasant, the driver had asked if this was her first visit to New York, and after she said yes, he was great to point out interesting landmarks to her. He frowned as they entered the neighborhood of her hotel. "This isn't the best area. Are you sure you don't want to find other lodgings? I'll take you somewhere else for no extra charge."

Kaylee stared out the window at the dirty streets, the bars on the windows of businesses and dwellings alike, and the groups of rough looking people standing around—smoking, arguing, staring back at her. This had been the only hotel she could afford that was close to Mama C's old school. She bit her lip. "I...I'll be okay. I don't plan on being out after dark." The confidence she'd exhibited when telling Blayne that same thing, now felt like melting slush on the side of a dirt road.

"Okay, if you're sure." He turned right and pulled up to a drop off area in front of a seedy looking hotel—only half of the lights on the sign out front lit up. "At least let me carry your bag inside for you." He didn't wait for her to answer. He turned off the engine, got her bag out of the back, and walked with her into the hotel lobby.

"Thank you," she smiled at him. "I really appreciate it."

"You're welcome. Please be careful."

She laughed nervously. "Now you sound like my boy...my *friend.* I'll be careful."

When she got to her room, she latched the door with all the locks provided. She wrinkled her nose as she inspected the small space. "I hope I don't get bedbugs." The place had a musty, moldy odor about it. The tiny bathroom proved where that smell came from. Mold climbed up the shower tile and onto the ceiling. "Or some sort of fungal disease."

She'd planned on going for a walk to find somewhere to eat dinner, but her heart raced at the thought of stepping outside alone. Maybe Blayne had been right to be worried. She ended up calling a delivery service and eating a cold burger and fries on the bed while she watched the news on the twenty-four-inch TV.

Kaylee stared out the window at the brick wall of the building next door. She shivered as she realized the frost on the window was on the inside as well as the outside. The old radiator rattled to life when she turned the heat up.

She took a deep breath to settle her nerves before dialing Blayne's number.

"Hello," he answered on the first ring.

"Hi." Kaylee tried to infuse a fake "everything's fine" tone into her voice. It didn't work.

"What's wrong?"

"Nothing. Just feeling a little out of my element."

"Are you sure that's all it is? How's the hotel?" Blayne asked, his voice rising a notch in suspicion.

The concern in his voice almost broke her. She pulled the phone away from her face and took a few breaths, holding back tears. When she put the phone back to her ear, Blayne said, "Are you still there? Is everything okay?"

"I'm here." *Dammit!* Her voice broke. She cleared her throat—maybe he'd think it was just because she had mucus in her throat. "The, uh, hotel is okay. A little run down, but that's all I could afford."

"Kaylee, are you sure you're alright?"

She didn't want him to worry or to be able to tell her "I told you so," so she dug deep and pulled off a good semblance of confidence in her voice. "I'm fine. I'll only be here for two nights. It's just been a long day."

"Okay. If you say so."

"I say so," she said. "I think I'm just going to go to bed now. I'll text you in the morning when I head over to the school."

"Alright. Don't forget," he said. "And, Kaylee?"

"Yeah?"

"Be careful. I..." He cleared his throat. "I really care about you."

Her throat closed up with emotion so she could only utter a whispered, "I care about you, too."

She lay down fully clothed on top of the sheets, hoping to stave off any bed bugs that might want to feast on her.

Kaylee slept fitfully and woke early. Her goal with showering was to get done as quickly as possible without touching the tile or shower curtain with any part of her body. The quick part proved to be easy, since there was no hot water.

Deciding to skip breakfast, she ordered a ride-share car to come pick her up and take her to the school where Mama C had taught. The car delivered her to an old brick building lined up on the street with businesses and hotels/residences made from the same brick. The front wall and front door were right up against the sidewalk. So different from the high schools Kaylee was used to back in Colorado.

She steeled herself and stepped through the front door to be met by a resource officer. "Young lady," he said, looking down at her, "you're late for class."

"Oh, umm," she stammered. "I'm not a student."

"No?" he questioned. "Then what's your business here?"

She probably should have thought this through better, maybe called ahead. "I am a college student, from Colorado, and I just need to talk to one of the secretaries and a couple of the teachers about my thesis project."

He raised an eyebrow. "Can I see your I.D.?"

She fumbled for her phone and slipped her Driver's License out of the phone case and handed it to him.

"And," he took the license from her, staring down at it. "What kind of 'thesis' brings you to this generic high school in New York, Miss Burke?"

A thought struck her. "How long have you been at this school,"—she glanced at his name tag—"Officer Weyland?"

He narrowed his eyes at her. "Almost twenty years. Why?"

Excited words came bubbling out of her. "My thesis project, it's about...well based on...a homeless woman and the family-like group she's formed with young adults in the streets of...well, the streets.

This woman, Mama C, she used to work here. Maybe you knew her. Her name is Claire—"

"Watson," the resource officer finished for her.

"Yes!"

"Claire's homeless?" Wrinkles appeared on his forehead.

Kaylee looked at her shoes and lowered her voice, the excitement at finding someone who knew Mama C dampened. "Unfortunately, yes."

"I think I need to hear the whole story. Follow me." Officer Weyland led her into the office where he leaned on the counter and said, "Lindsay, will you call Mrs. Jones and Ms. Owens to the office, please. Then the three of you meet us in the teacher's lounge."

He didn't wait for an answer, instead leading Kaylee back through the office into a small, dingy lounge. "Coffee?" he asked.

She rubbed her hand absently across her abdomen, trying to decide if coffee would help or make worse the roiling going on inside her. "No, thank you."

"Have a seat." He motioned to a plastic chair across from where he stood at the coffee maker. "I have a lot of questions, but we'll wait until the others get here so you don't have to tell your story twice."

Kaylee nodded and sat, thoughts running around in her head like ants with too much caffeine. She stood as the secretary entered with two other women.

"Lindsay, Beth, Sarah—this is Kaylee Burke," the officer said.

Kaylee reached for Lindsay's hand and, shaking it, said, "I think we spoke on the phone last week." The secretary nodded and looked up at Officer Weyland. Kaylee shook hands with the two teachers. They shut the door behind them and all found seats.

Officer Weyland spoke first. "Kaylee here has some news, and some questions I assume, about Claire Watson."

The only one who didn't look surprised was Lindsay.

Kaylee reached into her jacket pocket, then stopped. "Can I... Is it okay if I take some notes?"

The others looked at each other, then her, and nodded.

With a quiet sigh of relief, she pulled the notebook and pen out of her pocket and flipped it open to the page she'd written her questions on. She looked up at four expectant faces, sweat broke out on her forehead and her voice quavered a little as she spoke. "Okay...umm...did you all know Mama...I mean, Mrs. Watson well?"

Beth raised an eyebrow when Kaylee slipped and said "mama." But she answered first. "The four of us were inseparable here at school."

"And we got together once a month to play Bunko," Sarah said.

"What is going on?" Lindsay asked. Brow furrowed. "Where is Claire?"

"I'm not sure she wants...actually, I'm pretty sure, positive really, that she doesn't want anyone to know where she is." She hurried to continue before the three growly-faced ladies could let her have it. "But I can tell you she's homeless and has been that way for nine or ten years."

There was a collective gasp from the women, Mama C's old friends, then the questions came rapidly and in three different voices. "Is she okay?" "Is she crazy?" "Where is she?" Again.

Kaylee raised a hand, palm forward and waited for the storm to calm. "Can I ask some questions first and then I'll answer yours as best I can? Please?"

Beth settle back into her chair with a quiet huff. "Fine. But you'd better answer our questions, starting with why you're here."

Leaning forward slightly, Kaylee explained again about her thesis before beginning her questioning. "So, what was Mrs. Watson like, before the fire?"

Lindsay and Sara looked at Beth. "You were her bestie, you answer," Sara said.

With a nod, Beth started. "She was an angel. Don't get me wrong, she was strict, the strictest teacher of all of us. But the kids loved her anyway. She had a way of getting to the troubled students. Getting to them and forcing all the good in them up to the surface so the bad choked on it." She shook her head. "It was magical, watching her do her thing with these kids."

Sara nodded, wiping at a tear leaving a trail of dark mascara on her cheek. "It doesn't surprise me at all that she's taken some young homeless kids under her wing."

Beth laid her hand on top of Sara's and continued. "And boy oh boy did she love that husband and son of hers. Danny put that woman on a pedestal and she did everything within her power to keep him happy. Their son, Eugene, he was a bright boy. They had him later in life and Claire proclaimed him a miracle from the day she found out she was pregnant at age thirty-seven. He got a scholarship, an academic one, to Syracuse. Would have moved there that fall if..." Lindsay handed her a tissue.

Officer Weyland took over from her. "She loved that boy like no mother before her. Every morning she'd come in and have coffee with me and talk about Eugene. How he wanted to be a scientist and help find a cure for childhood cancer. How he volunteered at the children's hospitals whenever he had time. She was so proud when he got a full scholarship to Syracuse."

Kaylee wanted to ask about the fire, but she couldn't get her voice to work. She pictured the three of them—Mama C, Daniel, and Eugene—celebrating his achievements. How happy and proud she must have been.

"The fire," Lindsay spoke in a near whisper. "It was horrible. I was here, in the office, when the police came to tell her." Her eyes glassed over with the memory. "You could hear her screams all the way out in the yard."

Silence filled the room, except for the sniffling and quiet, choked sobs being released after ten years of being stifled. Kaylee let the tears roll freely down her face until Lindsay handed the tissue box to her. "And after? What did she do after the fire?" Kaylee uttered.

Beth blew her nose, took a deep breath. "She died. Right along with them." She glanced up at Kaylee, narrowed her eyes. "Oh, her body was alive. But she was just an empty shell. Her eyes grew dull and uninterested. Them dying sucked the soul right out of her. I'll never forget what she said when I asked her what she was going to do, since she'd spent all the life insurance money on the funerals. I asked her how she was going to live. She said, 'Doesn't matter. I'm just living to die now.'"

Voice hoarse, Lindsay said, "She had no other family. The landlord put her up in a hotel. She locked herself inside it for two weeks after the funeral. I don't think she even ate. She tried to come back to work after. I don't think she knew what else to do. But her first day back, one of her students came to the office, face pale, and whispered to me that Mrs. Watson was just sitting there, staring at the ceiling, tears falling on the papers on her desk. The kids didn't know what to do."

"Then she left," Officer Weyland said. "Walked right out the front door without saying a word. We never saw or heard from her again."

Silence engulfed them once more. It lasted until a tall black man burst through the door like Kramer on Seinfeld. He stopped short as he looked from one crying woman to the next, finally landing his gaze on Officer Weyland. "Everything okay in here, Karl?"

"Everything's fine, Mr. Johnson. We'll just be a few more minutes, if you don't mind telling the other teachers to give us some privacy for that long, I'd appreciate it."

"Yeah," he glanced around the somber room again, "yeah, no problem. I'll station myself right outside the door."

Kaylee cleared her throat. "Well, you answered all my questions without me even asking. What do you want to know from me?"

Beth leaned forward, her eyes drilling into Kaylee's. "Where is she?"

"She's..." Kaylee looked down at her hands, wringing in her lap. "She's in Colorado. She's helped so many young people get off the streets. But she refuses to get off the streets herself. She won't talk about her past—I had to turn into an amateur sleuth to figure out what I did."

"Colorado." Sara hissed through her teeth. "It's got to be mighty cold there. Please tell me she at least stays in a shelter."

Kaylee shook her head. "She won't. She stays under a viaduct, with her small, protective army of kids. I've supplied them all with warm sleeping bags. They have a place for a fire. She buys them food with the money from her retirement checks." Kaylee sighed. "She's the most stubborn person I think I've ever met."

The three women laughed and nodded. "How's her health?" Beth asked.

Kaylee shook her head. "It was good—up until a few weeks ago. She's developed a cough. I've been bringing her soup and medicine. My roommate's boyfriend is a resident, medical student, and he got some antibiotics for her, but he said she needs to be in a hospital."

"Maybe," Beth looked down at the tissue in her hand, "if one of us...if *I* could come and talk to her, maybe I could talk her into going to the hospital."

Kaylee's voice softened. "She is going to be extremely angry with me for looking into her past. That was the one rule she had when she relented to speak with me—no questions about her past. But I'll take any help I can get to convince her to go to the hospital." She thought for a moment. "How about you give me your number? When I get back tomorrow and go check on Mama C, I'll call you and hand her the phone. Maybe she won't hang up on you."

Beth smiled beneath her tears. "That would be wonderful." She leaned forward and took Kaylee's hands in hers. "Thank you, Kaylee."

CHAPTER 18

The weather had changed drastically in the hour she'd spent in the school. Kaylee zipped her coat and wound her scarf tighter around her neck. She turned away from the glass doors and toward Officer Weyland as she pulled her gloves on. "I'd like to get some authentic New York pizza while I'm here. Any suggestions?"

A wide smile brightened his face. "Well Miss Burke, that is something I can help you with for sure!" He pulled a small notebook and pen out of his shirt pocket and wrote as he talked. "Scarr's is my personal favorite, and it's not far from here. My wife prefers Nunzio's in Staten Island, but that's about a half-hour subway ride from here."

"Scarr's it is then." Kaylee took the paper from his proffered hand and stuffed it into her coat pocket. "Thanks for all your help, Officer Weyland. I'll be sure to let you know how Mama C is when I get back."

She stepped out to the sidewalk, wishing she'd remembered to bring her ski hat as snowflakes fell from the graying sky. She sighed and pulled her right glove off so she could punch the address for Scarr's into her phone. It was only a couple of miles away. She could walk since it wouldn't be open for a while yet, anyway. She put her glove back on then turned in the direction her map showed and had taken a few steps when her phone buzzed in her hand.

Blayne: *Hey, is everything okay*

Kaylee pulled her glove off with her teeth and shoved it in her pocket before answering. *Yes. I'm just leaving the school. I'm going to get some pizza.*

Blayne: *Why didn't you text this morning? You said you'd text me before you left to go to the school*

Her lips quirked up into a slight smile at his worry for her. *I'm sorry. I realized when I got up that it would be really early in Colorado and I didn't want to wake you up.*

Blayne: *I'm homeless and sleeping under a bridge I get up at around 4 every day cause that's when I start to really get cold Innocent college girl*

She pictured him rolling his eyes at her and ended up rolling her own eyes at herself. *Sorry, I didn't think about that.*

Blayne: *Well enjoy your pizza and call or text when you get back to the hotel safe and sound*

Kaylee: *I will.*

The cold air bit at her exposed hand, and she fumbled to pull her glove back on, promising herself she wouldn't remove it again until she was seated inside a warm pizza place. As she walked, she kept her head down, staring at the pavement of the sidewalk. She knew it was better to look up and stare your surroundings straight in the face, but it was cold. She didn't want to admit it to herself, but she was not *scared* so much, but maybe apprehensive? She'd always thought Denver was a big city, but this...it was unbelievable. Cars honking, people fast-walking down the sidewalks, sirens, construction, no one obeying the "walk-don't walk" signals. And the homeless. So many homeless people laying or sitting on the sidewalk, in the alleyways, in the alcoves of closed businesses. Cardboard box shelters. No shelter. Worn coats, fingerless gloves. No coats or gloves or hats. It all hit too close to home. And Kaylee wanted to help them, all of them. But knowing that she couldn't, she just tucked her head and speed-walked, following the directions on her phone. Just like everyone else surrounding her. If you can't help, then you ignore—is that how it was?

She couldn't accept that and knew she could help a little bit. She squared her shoulders and lifted her head. An old man in a ratted denim jacket leaned against a streetlight, shivering, a tattered foam coffee cup at his side. She slowed her walk and looked him in the eyes with a smile and a nod as she passed. The corner of his mouth turned up slightly, and he nodded back. She did this each time she saw someone like him on her route, thinking that maybe just being treated like a human being for a fleeting moment would brighten some of their days.

She reached the pizza place just as the owner flipped the "open" sign around and unlocked the door. She sat on a barstool at the counter so she could take advantage of the warmth wafting from the kitchen, and ordered a slice of pepperoni to eat there and two large pizzas to go. She pulled her notebook out and looked over her notes, adding to them as thoughts entered her mind. The smell of pepperoni, melting cheese, and baking pizza crust drifted to her, making her stomach growl in anticipation.

When the guy now working the counter finally slid a plate in front of her, the aroma was like what she thought heaven must smell like. At least the "food" part of heaven.

"Be careful, it's hot," the man said.

Kaylee looked at the napkin next to the plate then asked, "Do you have a fork?"

"A *fork*?" He folded his arms. "You aren't from around here, are you?"

"N...no. I'm from Colorado."

"Well, I'll get ya' a fork if you want, but around here we fold our slices in half and eat them like pizza was meant to be eaten."

"Isn't that messy?"

He laughed. "Only if the pizza is any good. That's why we give you a big napkin."

"Okay then." She shoved her notebook back inside her bag and folded the large slice in half. Cheese and grease dripped out of the front of it as she lifted it to her mouth. Burning her tongue was so worth it. She savored every messy bite, stopping only to drink from the can of soda she'd ordered along with it and to talk to the guy at the counter.

"So, what brings you to New York?" he asked.

Kaylee swallowed the large bite of pizza. "A thesis project. I just needed to talk to some people who weren't too keen on talking to me by phone."

He nodded. "How long are you staying?"

"I leave tomorrow. It was a short trip, and I have to get back before this semester starts." She turned to look out the windows facing the street. "I'd love to come back for a longer visit. Just with... someone else. Not by myself. And I'd prefer to stay in a better hotel," Kaylee mumbled.

"Well," he wiped down the counter then wiped his hands on his white apron. "I'm glad you're enjoying the slice and maybe you can stop back by when you visit again...with *someone*." He winked and smiled then moved down the counter to help a group of customers who'd just come in from the cold.

She finished her pizza with a smile on her face as she imagined walking the streets of New York with Blayne. Hand in hand. Stopping to take pictures in front of Time's Square, the Empire State Building, the 9/11 memorial. Her heart fluttered at the thoughts.

Warmth rushed up her neck as her imaginings were interrupted by the counter guy sliding two large pizza boxes next to her. "Here's your to-go order. You must be hungry."

Before she could answer, he hurried off to help more customers. The lunch crowd had arrived in force.

Kaylee bundled herself back up to go out into the cold, then grabbed the pizzas and headed out the door. She retraced her earlier steps back toward the school, stopping at each homeless person she came across to offer them a slice of pizza. She knew it wasn't much, but it was something. *Like throwing starfish back into the ocean,* she thought, remembering a story her grandma had told her when she was young. *I can't save all the starfish, but I can save this one.*

By the time she neared the school again, the pizza was gone and kids streamed out the doors. *What should I do now?* She didn't want to go back to the wretched hotel just yet—the idea of spending all evening there was not a pleasant one. As long as she got in before dark, she'd be okay.

"Siri, what are some nearby sites I can visit?" Kaylee asked into her phone.

A list popped up and Kaylee zeroed in on one in particular, the Lower East Side Tenement Museum. It was unlikely that she would be able to get a tour with such short notice, not to mention they were kind of expensive for her small budget, but she could wander through the gift shop and visitor's center and around the neighborhood. She clicked on the directions and followed the map.

The visitor's center proved to only make her wish she'd planned ahead and booked a tour. She was able to watch a video about some people who had lived there and the truly rough times they'd faced. She bought a book about the history of the museum, tucking it into her bag while thinking about how long it was going to take her to pay off her credit card. Looking at the time on her phone, she decided she'd have about an hour to walk around the area before it started to get dark, then she'd arrange a ride back to the hotel.

She followed a sign reading "Essex Market." There were so many shops! She wanted to visit each one and sample the food there, but there were just too many. The pizza she'd eaten before noon was starting to wear off, and she found herself struggling in earnest to make a decision of which of the small eateries to try for an early dinner. Kaylee decided on the Japanese deli, where she got a bento box and a sushi roll.

Strolling back outside after eating, Kaylee intended to explore just a few more shops, maybe get some ice cream, but it had already started to get dark. The cloud cover had been dreary and had hidden the sun all day, but now, it looked like someone had flipped the light switch off. She pulled her phone out. Five-thirty. She clicked on the ride-share app and was dismayed to see that the only available car was miles away from her location. She booked it and decided to explore a little more while she waited the estimated thirty minutes for it to arrive.

Streetlights lit the way, and the sky darkened to a deep black. Kaylee waited outside the Japanese deli for her ride. She looked at the app, her stomach churning as she saw that her ride was running late and wouldn't be there for another fifteen minutes. She stomped her feet and shoved her gloved hands into her pockets, tucking her chin down into her scarf. The temperature had dropped along with the sun. "I hope this driver has his heater turned up full blast," she mumbled.

Finally, the car pulled up to the sidewalk, Kaylee verified the license plate and driver's information, and climbed in. She buckled her seatbelt then pulled her scarf from around her mouth.

"Sorry I was late," the male driver said. "Traffic is bad at this time of day, but was even worse than expected tonight."

"That's okay," Kaylee said. "I'm just glad your car is warm." Her thoughts flitted back to the homeless people she'd fed earlier. They must be freezing.

"It's going to take longer to get to your hotel than usual, too. I hope you aren't in a hurry."

"No. I don't have any plans other than sleeping," *on filthy sheets,* she thought.

The driver pulled out into the street and turned his music up without bothering to ask her if this genre was okay with her. He was definitely not as customer aware as her driver from the airport. He was right about traffic though. The streets were slow-moving and packed. It was after eight by the time they reached the neighborhood where the hotel was.

"Mind if I drop you off here?" he said. "I have another gig I need to get to, and I need to turn here."

She drew in a breath to protest, they were still two blocks away from the hotel. And it was dark. And the streets were not well lit. But he'd pulled to the side and stopped the car, double parking, and the cab behind them had already started to honk.

Two blocks. She'd be fine. Kaylee had barely stepped out of the car, one foot between two parked cars, and the bad-mannered driver pulled away, squealing his tires as he sped around the corner. Kaylee shoved her hands in her pockets, glad that her bag hung around her shoulder, hidden underneath her coat.

Despite her aching feet, she walked fast, her heart rate speeding up and her instincts telling her to go faster. But she looked straight ahead and forced herself not to break into a run. Half a block from where she'd been dropped off, a man stepped out of the shadows of an overhang and matched her steps beside her.

"Why you in such a big hurry?" His raspy voice reminded her of all the boogie-men in all the scary movies she'd ever watched.

She ignored him and sped up.

"Hey sweetheart, no need to be rude. I just want to talk. Don't often see a pretty young thing like you on this street after dark."

"I'm sorry." Why did she say that? She swallowed. "I am in a hurry and don't have time to talk." She moved sideways, now walking on the curb next to the street. Her eyes darted up ahead and to the sides, finding no lights or open businesses for at least another block. She silently cursed the driver who had dropped her off on such a dark street.

The guy grabbed her arm and pulled her toward him, his face close enough to hers that she could smell his fetid breath. "Now, be nice. Smile. I ain't gonna hurt you." The glint in his eyes and sneer on his lips spoke otherwise.

Kaylee tried to jerk her arm out of his grasp, but his hold on her was tight. "Let go!"

"How about we go back here in this little alley so we can have some privacy. Get to know each other." He winked as he pulled her closer to a narrow space between two buildings.

She dug her feet in and pulled toward the street, yelling, "Let go! Someone help!"

Headlights flooded the road up ahead and Kaylee waved her free arm and continued to fight to loosen the man's grip. The car stopped alongside them, blue and red lights lighting up on top of it. The man let go and took off, and Kaylee fell into the side of the police car, slamming her shoulder into it.

The officer stepped out on the other side. "You okay, ma'am?"

All the adrenaline that had built up over the last few minutes released all at once and tore out of her in the form of tears. Her throat closed up and all she could do was nod as she pushed off the car to stand up.

"You really shouldn't be out here alone after dark. Or even when it's light out. This is a bad neighborhood." He walked around the front of his car and stood in front of her. "Where are you headed?"

Tears froze to her cheeks as she sniffed. Her voice came out shaky and shrill as she pointed down the street. "The hotel down there. The driver, he dropped me off back there." She gestured down the street in the opposite direction.

The officer narrowed his eyes angrily. "Damn ride-share drivers! He should have known better." He looked her over and asked, "Are you sure you're okay?"

Kaylee held to her right shoulder with her left hand. It still throbbed where she'd smacked into his car. "I'm okay. I just want to get to the hotel and go to sleep. My flight leaves early tomorrow." *Thank goodness.*

"Alright. Get in." He held the door open for her. "You can sit in the front seat. No way I'm letting you walk the rest of the way."

"Thank you." A sudden, profound weakness hit her like a brick. "I don't think I could walk right now."

Once inside the room, she locked and rechecked every lock on the door before collapsing onto the bed. Her phone buzzed in her pocket, a call this time, not a text, and she pulled it out and answered before thinking. "Hello?" She cringed as her voice came out high-pitched and tremulous.

"Kaylee," Blayne's deep voice both calmed her and brought back the terror she'd just experienced. "What's wrong?"

Words flooded from her mouth like a burst dam, all jumbled and incoherent like her thoughts. "The driver, he was late. It got dark and he...he dropped me off. I had to walk. It was dark. So dark. A man grabbed me. He tried to...to pull me into the alley. A cop stopped. My shoulder hurts. I'm okay. I'm okay." She covered her mouth to stifle a sob.

Blayne's voice deepened to a near growl. "*Are* you okay? Which ride-share did you use? What was the driver's name?"

Kaylee took a shuddering breath. "I...I think I'm okay. I hit my shoulder on the cop car." She paused to gain some semblance of control of her shaking voice. "I'll screenshot the info to you. I...I can't remember right now."

"Where are you?"

"In my hotel room. I'm okay. Just shaken."

In the background she heard who she thought was Hannah and Demarcus arguing over whose turn it was to go find wood for the fire, and a hacking cough that could only be Mama C. Blayne's voice softened as his footsteps crunched away from the sounds at the viaduct. "Kaylee. I'm so sorry this happened to you." She heard a whistle as he sucked air in through what was probably clenched teeth. "I..."

"You don't have to say 'I told you so'," she sighed. "I know, I should have listened to you. I should have checked out this area before booking this stupid, cheap hotel." She swiped angrily at the tears that refused to stop falling. In a quieter, still trembling voice, she said, "I just want to go home."

"I wasn't going to say 'I told you so.' I was maybe going to say 'you should have listened to me' but not 'I told you so.'"

Kaylee's voice cracked in a half-laugh, half-cry.

"But seriously," Blayne said, "you're coming home tomorrow, right? What can I do right now to help you?"

She nodded before realizing he couldn't see her. "I leave for the airport at five a.m."

"What can I do?" he repeated.

"Stay on the phone with me."

"All night if you want."

A relieved sigh blew through her lips. "Okay. Good. Good. But you sound cold, so please go back by the fire. I'm going to go brush my teeth, so hold on."

She set the phone on the bed and rushed through the tooth brushing process. "Are you still there?" She hated the fear that still touched her voice like a broken bow against a violin.

"I'm here. Try to get some sleep. I'll stay on the line as long as my battery lasts. It's fully charged now, so it should last a while."

Kaylee settled down on top of the covers, wincing as her head touched the pillow, thinking of lice and bed bugs. "I'll try. Talk to me. Please. Your voice is calming." Why did she say that? He probably thought she was so weak. And weird.

"Okay. Anything in particular you want me to talk about?" She heard no judgment in his voice.

"Anything. Your childhood. Your job. Your dreams and aspirations."

Blayne snorted. "I didn't have any dreams or aspirations until a month and a half ago. You brought hope back into my life."

"How romantic," Hannah sounded in the distance.

"Leave him alone, Hannah," Mama C warned, before her words were lost in a fit of coughing.

"Privacy is a problem on the streets," Blayne said, annoyed. "But, seriously. I owe you a lot, Kaylee."

"I didn't do anything for you that you couldn't have done on your own," she protested.

"Ahh, but there's the core of it. I *could* have done it on my own, but I *wouldn't* have. You gave me hope. And your belief in me gave me the confidence to move forward. I owe my life to you and Mama C."

She didn't know what to say. She decided she'd let him have this one. "I'm glad I stumbled into your life when I did then. And don't forget—you literally saved my life the first night we met."

"Oh, yeah, college girl," he growled in imitation of how he'd spoken to her the first couple of times they'd met.

Yawning, Kaylee rolled over and tucked the phone between her ear and the pillow.

"You sound exhausted. Try to go to sleep while I talk." Blayne's smooth voice calmed her like the slap of ocean waves against the shore. "I've been looking around for a place to rent. I almost gave up, I need to stay downtown and the rent there is outrageous. But a guy I work with has been combing the internet for me and he found a couple of places within my price range. Mostly just single rooms for rent or small—very small—studio apartments. But, you know, beggars can't be choosers." He laughed.

"Mmm hmm." Kaylee's eyes grew heavy, and she closed them. The adrenaline had finally worked its way out of her system.

"I'm going to go look at a couple tomorrow. I should have enough cash for a deposit and first month's rent with tomorrow's paycheck."

Kaylee drifted off to sleep with the sound of his voice in her ear.

She fumbled to find her phone in the mess of pillows as the alarm sounded at 4:30 a.m. Groaning, she punched the screen with her thumb to shut the blasted thing off. She sat up abruptly, a pain shooting through her shoulder, and opened her eyes wider. Putting the phone to her ear, she whispered, "Blayne?"

"Still here," he answered. He sounded wide awake.

"Did you get any sleep at all?"

"No. I wanted to be here in case you woke up."

Kaylee's heart stuttered, and she whispered, "Thank you."

"I'd do anything for you, Kaylee." And she knew he meant it.

CHAPTER 19

Kaylee watched from the airport window as the sky lightened with the rising sun. Her thoughts had run wild on the ride there, dark thoughts of what could have happened in the alley last night, to tender thoughts of Blayne. Now her mind was firmly settled on Blayne. He'd stayed on the phone all night. And he'd stayed awake just in case she woke up. Oh no! Had she snored? Did he hear her snore? Or worse, *fart* in her sleep? A rush of heat blossomed up her neck and face and she lowered her head so the other airport patrons wouldn't see the embarrassed blush.

But he'd stayed on the phone all night. Her throat tightened, and she pressed a hand to her chest. He'd stayed awake in case she needed him. His voice—just the sound of his voice—had calmed her terror.

She texted him when she got seated on the plane, even though he should still be sleeping. *On the plane. Thank you for last night. It meant so much to me. See you tonight.*

The phone buzzed in her hand before she had a chance to switch it to airplane mode.

Blayne: *You're welcome have a safe flight*

It would be a long day, with a four-hour layover in Chicago, she wouldn't be home until early evening. Kaylee smiled as she tucked her phone away in her pocket. She started to watch a movie on the seat-screen in front of her, but fell asleep shortly after the plane took off.

The landing was a little rough; Kaylee gripped the armrests and squeezed her eyes shut. She texted Allie with slightly shaking hands: *Just landed. I hope you remembered to come pick me up.*

Her heart rate had slowed to normal by the time the huge airplane pulled up to the gate, but she bit her lip in worry that Allie hadn't texted her back yet. Kaylee grabbed her purse and carry-on and stood in the aisle, waiting for the line to move. Her phone buzzed as she disembarked and she breathed a sigh of relief when she saw it was from Allie. *Of course I remembered! I just pulled in, let me know when you get to the pick-up area.*

Okay, Kaylee sent back.

She rushed to the train that would take her to the pick-up area, thoughts of seeing Blayne later causing a warmth to erupt in her chest, and what she was sure was a cheesy smile to spread across her face.

Going with the flow of the pushing and shoving passengers leaving the train, Kaylee fumbled with her phone to text Allie. She pushed send on her message, pocketed her phone, zipped up her coat, and headed for the exit to meet her friend—glad to be back in Denver.

The fading sunlight made the chill air feel even colder as it touched the bare skin of her face. She wished she'd pulled her scarf out of her suitcase before stepping outside. She looked up and down the row of vehicles waiting to pick people up and relaxed her shoulders when she spotted Allie standing next to her car, waving both hands above her head.

Hurrying to reach the warmth of the car while smiling and waving at Allie, Kaylee didn't see the man who stepped in front of her until she smashed into him and dropped the handle of her rolling suitcase.

"Oh, I'm so sorry!" She took a step back and her foot landed on the handle. She stumbled, letting out a little yelp as she fell toward the curb. A strong hand grabbed her arm and hauled her up, steadying her as she regained her balance. She looked up, preparing to spit an embarrassed thank you at the stranger before scurrying to the safety of Allie's car. Her breath caught in her throat as she realized the "stranger" was a smirking, breathtakingly handsome man. "Blayne! What are..."

With a deep chuckle he embraced her, cutting off her question. She stiffened at first, still confused at seeing him there, but as she breathed in his scent—a combination of campfire smoke and cheap laundry detergent—she relaxed into him and returned his hug.

Blayne laid his cheek on the top of her head and said in a low, husky voice, "I wanted to surprise you. Guess it worked, huh?"

She nodded against his chest and squeezed tighter as she remembered how he'd stayed on the phone with her all night.

"All right lovebirds! It's freezing out here and this parking attendant is giving me the evil eye. How about you get in the car?" Allie's loud voice seemed to echo all around them.

Kaylee didn't even care. And, for the first time since she could remember, she didn't feel the warm flush of an embarrassed blush creeping up her neck as the object of strangers' attention. The warmth she was feeling had nothing to do with embarrassment.

Blayne's biceps tightened around her arms for another couple of seconds before he released her. Still close enough to feel his warm breath on her face, she looked up and smiled at his one raised eyebrow.

He said, "I guess we'd better do as we're told before your friend decides to use her loud voice again."

Kaylee laughed, wanting nothing more than to kiss those lips quirked into a mischievous grin. Before she could act on this strong impulse, Blayne pulled away. He grabbed her hand as they walked the few yards to Allie's car.

"You two ride in the back," Allie said. "I'll pretend like I'm chauffeuring a celebrity couple around." She got in the driver's seat and turned to look at them as they buckled up. "And, bonus for both of us, I can't hear what you two lovebirds are talking about back there."

"She makes a good point." Blayne reached to hold her hand again as soon as both of their seatbelts were buckled.

The callouses on his palm rubbed against her 'college girl' skin and she thought how nothing had ever felt quite so good. "How is work going?" she asked.

"Great. I love my job and my coworkers. It's so good to be doing something productive with my life." His smile of moments before turned to a look of concern, his eyes tight as he gazed at her. "I'm so glad you're back. Safe." He pursed his lips like he had more to say, but held it back.

Kaylee looked down at their entwined fingers. "Me too. I'll never travel by myself again."

"I was so worried about you." A small hitch in his voice made her look up at him. His eyes bore into hers before he turned to look out the window. He rubbed the back of his neck. "That driver that dropped you off won't be doing that to anyone else. At least not with the same drive-share company."

Kaylee became acutely aware of every inch of her hand that touched his. His leg pressed up against hers in the crowded back seat of Allie's compact car. His breath blowing against the window, fogging the view. His shoulders, so broad they took up more than his share of the backrest, the arm next to her rubbing against her coat with each bump in the road. Her heart fluttered like a rose petal floating on a breeze. She squeezed his hand, staring at the back of his head, waiting for him to turn his face to her again.

When he did, the intensity of his gaze softened as she blinked up at him. "Thank you," she whispered.

He nodded in response, his eyes flicking to her lips then back to her gaze.

Kaylee cleared her throat and looked down at her lap again. She must look like a huge mess. She hadn't bothered to put makeup on that morning, she'd barely slept the night before, she'd slept on the plane, and she hadn't showered in well over twenty-four hours. She touched her hair, realizing pieces of it had escaped the scrunchy and now poked out everywhere. Ugh. Why hadn't she taken the time to freshen up in the bathroom at the airport?

She avoided Blayne's gaze the rest of the drive home, telling him what she'd found out about Mama C as she stared out the window.

ALLIE PULLED into her parking space at their apartment building and turned off the car. She turned in her seat to look at Kaylee. "I figure you can give Blayne a ride when he's ready to go."

Kaylee knew she was going to say "home" but stopped herself. A sleeping bag under a viaduct wasn't really a home, was it? "Thank you, Al."

Blayne touched Allie on the shoulder and when she looked at him, he signed, *Yes, thank you for letting me come with you to get Kaylee.*

Allie and Kaylee both opened their mouths in shock. "When did you learn how to sign?" Allie asked.

Blayne shrugged, his face turning a shade darker. "I just went to the library on my lunch breaks this week and taught myself a few words. I learned that sentence the day after you said I could come with you to the airport."

"Blayne that's..." Kaylee searched for the right words. "That's the sweetest thing."

His blush darkened further, and he mumbled, "It's no big deal."

With a slight tremor in her voice, Allie said, much quieter than usual for her, "It is a huge deal. You have no idea how much it means to me."

He shook his head, then must have decided not to object again. "Well, you're welcome. I don't know very much, but I'm going to try to keep learning."

Allie patted his cheek then turned back to open her door, swiping at her face as she did so.

Kaylee and Blayne stood next to the car as Allie climbed the stairs to their apartment. "Well, what's the plan? Are you hungry?" he asked.

She nodded. "I am. I haven't eaten all day." Her stomach growled in agreement. "Want to come in? I'll make you one of my famous peanut butter and jelly sandwiches."

His smile lit up his eyes. "I'd love that."

She stopped halfway up the stairs and turned to him with a frown. "I just realized that Allie-the-mess-maker has been home without me for three full days. The place could be a disaster. Probably is a disaster."

He tilted his head and cocked an eyebrow. "Do you really think I care about that?"

"No. But I just thought I'd warn you. In case you were under the impression that all college girls were neat freaks or something."

He laughed. "I've seen the inside of your car, remember?"

"Hey! A car isn't the same. I clean it out at least every six months whether it needs it or not."

He shook his head with a smirk and followed her the rest of the way up the stairs.

The apartment was indeed a mess. Kaylee cleared the couch of a pile of clothes so Blayne could sit down before she excused herself to go to the bathroom and whisper-yell at Allie for not cleaning up after herself.

Staring at herself in the mirror, she was horrified at how she looked. Hair a mess. Dark circles under her eyes. Yesterday's makeup smudged on her eyelids. She did what she could without taking a full-on shower. She scrubbed her face, brushed her hair and put it up into a messy bun, and applied a small amount of makeup to cover up the dark circles. It would have to do. Allie popped her head in and said with a wink, "Going to Max's. Behave yourself."

Kaylee made sandwiches while Blayne sat at the small kitchen table and talked to her. "So, what's the secret behind your 'famous' peanut butter sandwiches?"

"Can I trust you to keep a secret?"

"Of course you can," he said with a straight face.

"Okay then. The secret to the world's best peanut butter sandwich is that you triple the amount of peanut butter a normal human would use, but apply the normal amount of jelly." She plopped a paper-plated sandwich in front of him with a flourish, along with a can of soda. "You'll need something to wash that down with."

She grabbed her own plate and a bag of chips and sat across from him. "So, anything exciting happen while I was gone?"

He swallowed and took a drink of soda before answering. "Well, maybe."

She sat up straighter at the touch of excitement in his voice. "Spill it!"

Blayne laughed. "Okay. Okay. I found a place to live."

"That's fantastic!" Tears stung the backs of her eyes. She couldn't believe the progress he'd made.

"It's just a small studio. Very small. But it's within my price range and I have enough money saved up for the deposit and first month's rent. And it's furnished, sort of."

She raised her eyebrows. "Sort of?"

"It has most of what I need. A couch that folds out into a bed, a couple of bar stools, a stove, and small fridge, an old TV." He sighed dramatically. "But it doesn't have the most important appliance; a microwave. How am I supposed to make my gourmet microwave burritos without one? I might starve, actually."

"Hey, if mac and cheese and ramen noodles are good enough for the rest of us, they're good enough for you." She pointed a potato chip at him. "Microwave burritos are for the rich."

He frowned and put a hand on his chest. "Are...are you calling me a burrito snob?"

"I'm afraid so." She tried to keep her serious face, but the fake puppy-dog eyes he gave her were just too much. She laughed, and he joined her.

He helped her clean up and even took the garbage out without being asked. When he came back in, he said, "So, I'm supposed to go down and pay my deposit and stuff tomorrow afternoon. Will you hold on to this and what you already have until tomorrow?" He handed her a wad of cash.

"Of course. What time do you need to be there tomorrow?"

"Two o'clock." He looked down. "I was hoping that you would maybe consent to a second date." He raised his head and smiled shyly. "I was thinking we could go get lunch and then I could show you my new place. My treat."

"I'd love to. What time should I pick you up?"

"Noon?"

She nodded. "That works." She looked out the window at the darkening sky. "It's getting late. We should probably go check on Mama C." She really didn't want this evening to end. Didn't want to drop him off to sleep outside in the freezing cold. Knowing she'd see him again tomorrow gave her slight solace. But...words left her mouth before her brain could apply the brakes. "Why don't you stay here tonight?" Heat rushed to her face, and she hurried to clarify. "On the couch, I mean. Out of the cold."

He took her hand that wasn't holding the wad of cash he'd just given her and stared at her with soulful eyes. Beautiful blue eyes. "Thank you, Kaylee. Seriously, thank you for the offer. I appreciate it so much."

"But..." she said.

"But I can't. I need to make sure Mama and the kids are okay. It'll be my last night with them and I'm going to try my hardest to talk Mama into coming to stay with me—even though it would mean I'd have to sleep on the floor. Hell, I want them all to come stay with me, but there isn't room, and it's against the conditions of the lease. No more than two people allowed." He rubbed a hand across his face. "I'm having a hard time with this. I mean, I'm so happy to be finally moving forward with my life, but I don't want to leave them behind." His voice had lowered to a whisper.

Kaylee tightened her grip on his hand and she nodded wordlessly.

"Thank you for understanding." He held her gaze the way gravity held the moon in orbit.

Her mouth and throat went dry. She swallowed, trying to push a giant lump down. She croaked out, "I'm going to go put your money away."

They continued to stand that way for several more seconds until Blayne broke the spell he'd woven between them. He let go of her hand and cleared his throat. "Yeah. Yeah, good idea."

Slipping the cash in her sock drawer with the rest of it, she scolded herself. Why did she interrupt that moment? She knew why. She was scared. Scared and thrilled at the idea of a kiss. She hadn't kissed many boys in high school, and really no guys in college—unless you counted the peck on the cheek from the sweet Mormon kid who'd taken her to get ice cream her Freshman year. She just hadn't been interested in dating, her priority was school. Until now. She shook her head at her conflicting feelings. She really wanted Blayne to kiss her. Why was she so nervous? Stupid girl. She took a deep breath before going back out to him.

"Ready?" she asked.

He nodded and opened the door for her. He put his hand on the small of her back as they walked down the stairs—and even through her coat she felt a jolt of electricity spread throughout her body from his touch. She was in trouble. She wasn't falling for him, she had already fallen. Like an anchor to the bottom of the ocean.

CHAPTER 20

Mama C had looked better last night. No more fever, and her cough seemed to have calmed a little. She was still short of breath, though, and that worried Kaylee even though Max said it was normal.

The sun was out, and Kaylee smiled as she drove to the viaduct. Today would be Blayne's last homeless day. Her joy at seeing him succeed and pull his life together was dampened by thoughts of Mama C and the others. She frowned, needing a way to help them all.

Kaylee parked on the graveled area and got out. She patted her coat where Blayne's money lay hidden in an inside pocket—she didn't dare leave it in her car. Blayne stood, smiling, as she approached. She smiled back, then bent down to feel Mama C's forehead, nodding at the cool temperature of her skin. "How are you feeling?"

With a good-natured scowl, Mama C answered, "I'm fine. You all need to quit fussing over me."

"You're worth fussing over, Mama C." Kaylee straightened up and put her hands on her hips for emphasis.

Mama C waved a hand dismissively. "Psshh. You need to go on about your business, Miss Kaylee. Get that boy,"—she nodded toward Blayne—"into his new home. I'll be fine here, and if I'm not, well then, it's God's will."

Either at the mention of Blayne leaving or Mama C's indifference toward her own well-being, the mood shifted around them.

"Mama," Hannah said. "Don't talk like that. We need you.

Especially since Blayne is leaving us." There was a sulking tone to her voice to match the frown.

"Now Hannah." Mama C shook a finger at the girl. "Don't you be down about Blayne's accomplishments. Where he is now is where you all should be aiming." She looked around, stopping to gaze at each of them in turn. "And, you can. Each one of you." She nodded. "You're ready."

"Where are you aiming, Mama?" asked DeMarcus quietly.

Kaylee thought about what Beth had said about Mama C saying she was "just living to die" after the fire. She also remembered her promise to call Beth and let Mama talk to her. No time today. She'd do it soon.

The old woman sucked in a breath then coughed for a good thirty seconds before responding. "I'm aiming to whoop you if you don't quit getting into my business." Her voice softened as she said, "I'm going to keep doing what I've been doing for as long as the Lord allows. There are other kids out there that need help, you know. The world doesn't revolve around you all."

Kaylee glanced up at Blayne. His mouth turned down into a frown and she could read the worry in his eyes like the pages of a book.

Mama read it, too. "Blayne, this is a glorious day. Celebrate. Pay it forward when you can. Now go. You've got a beautiful girl waiting for you to feed her lunch."

Blayne flicked his eyes up at Kaylee and his lips twitched in an almost-smile. "Yes, I do." He bent down and hugged Mama C. "I'll be back later to check on you."

"Not one of you listens to a word I say," she mumbled.

Blayne fist bumped with Clint and DeMarcus, and one-arm-hugged Hannah. "Stay out of trouble. I'll be back to check on you frequently. If—or when—you move to a new location, make sure one of you meets me at the shelter so I know where you are."

Hannah turned her face away, wiping at her cheeks.

Looking at Kaylee, Blayne asked, "Are you ready?"

She nodded. He hefted his backpack onto his shoulder, leaving his rolled up sleeping bag where it lay.

Blayne leaned in to open her door for her. "Where do you want to eat?"

"You choose. It's your 'glorious day,' as Mama C said." She smiled with a closed mouth and ran her hand along his stubbly cheek. The difficulty he was having with leaving his make-shift family was understandable, and she wanted him to feel her support.

One side of his face twisted up into a sad smile and he trapped her hand against his face under his hand. Her breath caught at his touch and she was again spellbound by his gaze. He brought her hand to his lips and kissed it, his mouth then blossoming into a full smile that almost reached his eyes. "Let's go all out, then. Sizzler it is." He wiggled his eyebrows and squeezed her hand before letting go to walk to the passenger side of the car.

At lunch they talked about what classes Kaylee was taking this, her last, semester that started in two days. They talked about what items Blayne would need for his new place. But they steered clear of discussing the scene at the viaduct and Blayne's obvious guilt at moving on.

Kaylee insisted on leaving the tip for their server before they headed out to meet the landlord. In the car she handed Blayne his money then drove as he guided her.

She parked in a small, torn up parking lot, more potholes than asphalt. "This isn't a very good neighborhood." Her mind flashed back to New York and her hands tightened on the steering wheel, her eyes shut tight.

"It's the best I—" Blayne laid his hand on hers. His tone softened. "Are you okay?"

She released a gush of air from her lungs, opened her eyes, and attempted to smile. "Yeah. Fine."

"You sure? You turned white as a ghost."

"I'm sure." She removed her hand from under his and unclipped her seatbelt. "Let's go meet your landlord." She opened the door and slid out of her seat before he could push her for an explanation.

Kaylee shut her door then absently grabbed her shoulder where she'd hurt it falling into the police car in New York. She leaned against her car and Blayne stood in front of her faster than should have been possible.

He dipped down to look into her eyes. "You are not okay. What's going on?"

The tenderness in his voice broke through her flashback wall. "I just... I don't know...suddenly thought about New York. The guy in the alley."

And then she was in his arms, her face pressed against his chest, eyes screwed shut to hold back the threatened waterworks. His warm breath on the top of her head calmed her. His arms wrapped tightly around her comforted and excited her.

"I'm fine," she mumbled. "It's stupid for me to be scared. This isn't New York."

"Don't apologize. It isn't stupid. And just because this isn't New York doesn't mean there isn't danger here—you already know that." He pulled away enough to look her in the eyes. "You don't have to come here again after today. I'll meet you somewhere else when—if—you want to see me."

Kaylee shook her head and got her voice back. "No. I'll come here *when* I want to see you. My reaction was ridiculous, especially considering the other places I've gone to see you." She smiled and rolled her eyes.

Cocking his head adorably to the side, Blayne returned her smile. "True. But still, I don't want you to...to think about that incident every time you come here."

"I won't." She nudged him with her shoulder. "Let's go, it's almost two o'clock."

After the lease was signed and money and keys exchanged, Blayne raised his eyebrows and said, "You ready to see *Chez* Blayne?"

"Oh, I didn't know you spoke French," she teased.

"There's a lot you don't know about me." He winked.

She raised her eyebrows. "That's the truth."

Blayne pulled her forward like a kid rushing to the tree on Christmas morning. They clanked up the metal steps that led to his new studio apartment. His hands shook as he inserted the key in the lock and twisted. The smile on his face as he ushered her inside warmed her heart. He took her coat and draped it over the back of the couch, doing the same with his.

The grand tour took only a minute, as the apartment consisted of one combined area for the kitchen and living room/bedroom, with a tiny bathroom off the living area. But it was clean. The sofa bed was a little worn but not terrible. It had heat. And it made Blayne beam. He rummaged through his backpack until he found his toothbrush and toothpaste. He dropped them on the tiny counter in the bathroom, then walked to the couch and deposited his backpack on it, stating, "There. I'm all moved in."

Kaylee laughed and tilted her head to the side, fully taking in the transformation of this man she'd come to care so deeply about.

"What are you laughing at?" Blayne asked, still smiling.

"You."

He wrapped his arms around her waist and lifted her into the air. She squealed as he twirled her around. "Put me down." Her demand didn't come across as too demanding, since she was giggling like a school girl.

He set her down, keeping his arms around her. His face barely an inch from hers, his smile faded, his forehead creased. "Kaylee." Her name left his lips like a sigh in the wind. Her stomach twisted in the most pleasant of ways and her face transformed to match the seriousness of his.

When his hands left her waist and cupped her face, she lost the ability to speak. When he sighed her name again, "Kaylee," deeper this time, like the sigh caught on something on its way out, she lost the ability to breathe. When he tilted her head back with the gentleness of a butterfly's wings, she lost the ability to think.

Blayne searched her eyes for a moment before slowly touching his lips to hers. She closed her eyes and rested her arms around his waist. His lips explored hers with a gentle touch, and she responded with a quiet moan. He drew in a sharp breath, one of his hands moved to the nape of her neck, pulling her in closer, increasing the pressure on their hungering lips. Kaylee's legs lost all strength and her head spun. Blayne moved his hands from her face down to wrap around her back. She clung to him like a lifeline, encircling her arms around his neck. Another moan formed deep in her throat, and she was powerless to stop it.

He ended the kiss as slowly as he started it. Pulling away with a shaky sigh, he kept one hand on the small of her back and stroked her face lightly with the other, resting his forehead on hers. The nerve endings where he touched her fired at warp speed, sending indescribable sensations coursing across her skin. Her breath came fast as she stared into his eyes. She wondered if her pupils were dilated like his. If her face was flushed like his. If his lips tingled like hers. If he wanted to do that all over again like she did.

"Can I do that again?" he asked, his voice choked with emotion.

She nodded, still unable to form words.

The light teasing of his lips on hers made her shiver. She tangled her fingers into his thick hair, tightening her grip with a spasm when the light teasing switched to crushing intensity. It was his turn to moan. That short, deep, purring sound made her heart beat out of control. One of his hands slid under her sweater, brushing against the tender, bare skin at the small of her back. She inhaled sharply at his touch, leaning into him. His tongue parted her lips and toyed with the tip of her tongue, traced the inside of her lips before retreating, leaving her wanting more.

This time when he pulled away, he crushed her to him, her cheek pressed against his heaving chest. Her rapid breaths matched his, and his heart beat erratically against her ear. He stroked her hair with a gentle touch, his lips pressed to the top of her head.

They stood that way for several minutes, just breathing in each other's scent, letting the tidal wave of sensations and emotions ebb.

Blayne slowly leaned away from her and tilted her chin up to stare into her eyes. "Kaylee," the roughness still in his voice spread warmth up her neck and face, "I think I'm in..." He blinked then cleared his throat. He dropped his hands from around her, then ran them through his hair. "I think we should go check on Mama C."

The change in his voice and demeanor hinted that that wasn't what he'd intended to say. What had he been going to say? Kaylee had an idea, but was she ready to hear those words from him?

CHAPTER 21

Kaylee had two classes on Monday morning. Reading through the syllabuses usually caused her great stress—thinking about all the work she'd have to get done that semester. But nothing could penetrate the post-kiss haze that engulfed her, body and soul. Blayne's lips had been everything she'd imagined all that time she'd spent staring at them. And more.

She sat in the library and absently ran her fingers over her lips, closing her eyes and reliving last night in her mind. After leaving his apartment, they'd gone back to check on Mama C. Even though it was early, she'd been sound asleep. Blayne had kissed Kaylee goodbye after he walked her back to her car. It was a quick, simple kiss, lacking the intensity of earlier—yet it still lit a firestorm of tingling that traveled from her lips to every inch of her wilting body.

The buzzing of her phone stirred her from her trance. She pulled it from her pocket and clicked the "home" button. It was a text from Blayne: *Wanna meet for lunch? I have 45 minutes*

Forty-five minutes is a long enough time to get more kissing in. Kaylee shook her head, smiling at the thought so unlike her. *What had he done to her?*

She texted back: *Sure! Meet at the student union?*

Blayne: *Yes see you in a few minutes*

Kaylee shoved her syllabuses in her bag then slung it over her shoulder, humming to herself and just barely able to resist the strong urge to skip all the way there. It was going to be great having Blayne work on campus.

Kaylee grabbed a salad and sat across from Blayne at one of the tables nearby. "How was the first night in your new home?"

Blayne finished chewing the bite of his sandwich he'd just taken and swallowed it down with a swig of water before answering. "It was great." His smile didn't quite reach his eyes.

Tipping her head to the side as she studied him, Kaylee said, "You don't seem like it was so great."

He shrugged. "I mean, it was great to sleep on a bed, in a warm apartment. It was great to take a shower and use the toilet."

"But..."

Another shrug. "It's just going to take some getting used to. Being alone. As much as I've longed for privacy over the last few years, I forgot how quiet it can be."

He looked down at his sandwich.

Softly, Kaylee dug a little deeper. "Are you feeling guilty about the others still being out in the cold?"

His lips pressed into a white slash. He pushed his hair back from his forehead, answering without looking at her. "Yeah. Of course I am. Wouldn't you be?"

The touch of sharpness to his tone stung. Kaylee put her fork down and breathed in to steady her voice. "Yes. I would and do. You have no idea how many times I've wished you all could just come and stay in my apartment."

He finally looked her in the eye, the lines of his face softening along with his voice. "I'm sorry. Of course you would." He grasped her hand across the table. "You're one of the best people I've ever met, and you don't deserve to be the object of my irritability."

She tightened her grip on his hand. "I've been thinking. Why can't I—or we—help them do what you've done? Or, since they're all so young, help them to go back home?"

A sad smile crossed his lips. "Mama C's been talking to me about that. She has some plans for us."

"She does, does she?" Kaylee smiled.

"Yep. But I'll let her tell you about them." He took a huge bite of his sandwich, a cue that the subject was closed for now.

When they'd both finished eating and thrown away their trash, Blayne took her hand and smiled down at her, a spark of mischief glowing in his eyes. "I have fifteen minutes before I have to be back. Wanna go find a quiet place and *talk*?"

Kaylee's mouth twisted as she tried not to smile. The way he said "talk"—she knew that wasn't what he meant. Her face flushed with warmth, and the tumbling of her insides urged her to answer. "Yes. I know a good place to *talk*."

She led him to a quiet corner, hidden from view under a set of stairs. She leaned her back against the wall, her breath quickening when he stepped close, facing her, holding both her hands in his at her sides. He stared into her eyes and stepped closer, his feet on either side of hers.

"So," her voice quivered as she looked up at his blue eyes, swimming with desire. "What did you want to talk about?"

"This." He tipped his head and caught her lips with his. And caught her breath with his. And caught her heart.

Her grip tightened around his fingers as realization tightened around her chest. She loved him. And that knowledge wrapped her up with both icy fear and gentle warmth. As their kiss intensified, the warmth took over, flooding her body with a surreal sensation of peace.

He released her hands and rested his palms on either side of her face, his fingers in her hair and thumbs on her cheeks, tilting her head up as the kiss deepened, stealing her breath away. She hugged him close, her mind a jumbled mess of sensations, unable to form a single coherent thought.

He pulled away, resting his forehead on hers as he'd done yesterday. Her lips felt inflamed and slightly swollen. Blayne breathed in a long draught of air, his gaze never leaving hers. "Kaylee," he breathed out, barely a hoarse whisper, "you are so amazing." His breath on her face hypnotized her. "I..." He pinched his eyes shut and exhaled sharply. "I should get back to work."

The spell broken, he dropped his hands, taking hers lightly in his as she unwrapped them from around his waist. He pressed his lips to hers one last time in a quick goodbye kiss.

They left their hidden corner and went together to the exit. Kaylee watched him walk away, headed back to the construction site, wondering again what he'd been about to say before he'd stopped himself.

She was going to have a hard time concentrating in her afternoon class. Then she had to TA after that. She touched her fingers to her lips. Best. Lunch. Ever.

AFTER KAYLEE'S TA duties were done, she headed over to the building that housed the surplus items the school was selling for cheap. Maybe they would have something she could get for Blayne as a housewarming gift. She spotted the perfect item right away—a small microwave. It looked clean. Hoping it hadn't been used in some lab rat experiment over in the science building, she purchased it for ten bucks and lugged it to her car.

Looking at the clock on her dashboard as she started the car, she realized that Blayne would probably be home from work. Her TA job went later than his construction job. She smiled, deciding to surprise him.

She pulled up to his building, parking near the steps leading up to his studio. She put the car in park and turned off the engine. Kaylee grabbed her phone and got out, lifting her hand to wave as she spotted Blayne partially hidden on the other side of the stairs, talking to someone, his back turned to her. She decided to leave the microwave in her car, not wanting to stand there holding it while he finished talking.

Taking a few steps in his direction, she stopped, narrowing her eyes. It didn't look like a friendly conversation. She could hear their raised voices, but not what they were saying. Blayne gestured angrily, and the other guy pointed at him then poked him in the chest hard enough that Blayne took a step back.

Kaylee hurried over. Blayne's back to her, she pasted on a smile as she approached. The guy glanced at her and shoved something in his pocket. He grinned, instantly sending creepy chills down her spine. "Well, hello there." He licked his lips, looking her up and down, then looked back at Blayne. "Who's this, Blayne?"

Blayne turned to her, face wrinkled in anger. His eyes widened slightly when he saw her and he swore under his breath. Turning away from her, he answered, "She's no one. Come on," he grabbed the guy's arm and pulled him away, down the street.

She couldn't breathe, he may as well have punched her in the gut. She stumbled back a step and wrapped her arms around her torso, trying to stop the hemorrhaging of her soul. Tears fell as she whipped around and staggered to her car. Her phone slipped from her hand and she barely registered it, leaving it on the ground.

Her front tires spit gravel as she sped out of the parking lot. She could barely see through the tears as she ugly-cried all the way back to her apartment. Allie's car was there, Kaylee couldn't decide if she was glad her friend was home or not.

After rushing up the stairs, her hands shook as she tried to unlock the door. Before she could even get the wobbling key in the lock, Allie opened it. Taking one look at Kaylee, she pulled her inside and into a hug.

"What happened?" her friend asked, pulling away so she could see Kaylee's lips as she answered.

Kaylee shook her head, her breath hitching as she tried to get ahold of herself. She went to the couch and sat, holding her stomach and rocking back and forth. As the shock wore off, anger quickly filled in.

Handing her a tissue, Allie sat next to her, angled so they could see each other's faces. She put a hand on Kaylee's knee and waited for her to talk.

Kaylee's words came out jumbled, just as they appeared in her brain. "He started to tell me something last night when we kissed. Then again today. But he stopped. I thought maybe..." She shook her head. "I'm so stupid!"

"I didn't catch all of that, your tissue was in the way. But I caught enough," Allie said. "But you are *not* stupid. Slow down and tell me what happened. And kiss? What kiss?"

Kaylee put her hands in her lap, tearing the tissue to shreds as she spoke. "He kissed me last night. And again today at lunch. Both times he tried to tell me something after, but stopped. I thought he was...I thought maybe he was going to," her hands balled into tight fists in her lap, "tell me how he felt about me."

"Okay?" Allie said. "I still don't understand why you're so upset."

"I went to his new apartment. I wanted to surprise him." She bit her bottom lip. "He was talking to a creepy guy. Blayne told him I was 'no one' then turned and walked away with him!"

"Oh. Wow. That doesn't sound like Blayne at all." Allie frowned.

"I know. Allie, what if he's back to his old behavior? What if having money for drugs was too tempting for him? Maybe that's what he was trying to tell me."

"No, Kay. That can't be it. You should give him a chance to explain. Have you heard from him?"

Kaylee shook her head. "You should have seen the look he gave me. Disgust. Maybe even fear. He was afraid I'd caught him at something, maybe?"

Allie set her lips in a stubborn line. "I don't believe that. You need to call him."

"No. I can't. He can call me if he wants to explain." She stood and hugged her friend. "I'm going to bed."

THE NIGHT WAS long and full of conflicting thoughts. It was probably a good thing Allie couldn't hear her crying and thrashing around in bed. Kaylee got up before her alarm went off—then realized her alarm, her phone, wasn't even there. "Shoot!" A vague memory of dropping it in the parking lot at Blayne's resurfaced. There was no way she could afford a new phone right now. And there was no way she was going to Blayne's to get it. Maybe she could talk Allie into going to look for it.

She got dressed, brushed her teeth, and rushed to class, throwing her hair into a messy bun on her way out to her car.

"You look rough this morning," her friend Jamie said as she plopped her bag down and slid into the chair beside her.

"Yeah. Rough night." Kaylee pulled a notebook and pen out of her bag and faced the front of the class, not wanting to talk to anyone.

KAYLEE STAYED LATE at the library, "studying" after class and TA-ing. She really just didn't want to go home. What had she expected? She knew falling for Blayne was a dangerous prospect. She knew the rate of relapse for drug addiction was high.

When she got home, she washed her face, brushed her teeth, then fell into bed. Allie rolled over in her bed across the room and flipped on her bedside lamp. "You're late. Have you even eaten anything today?"

Kaylee shook her head and rolled over to face the wall. After a few minutes of silence, Allie clicked the lamp off and scooted down into her sheets.

The next two days were much the same, except with more nagging from Allie, trying to get Kaylee to eat more and trying to get her to go talk to Blayne.

Just before dark on the third night after the incident, Kaylee decided to go check on Mama C. She felt a ton of guilt for not having done it sooner. It wasn't the older woman's fault, what had happened with Blayne, whatever that really was.

As Kaylee pulled into her spot near the viaduct, she hesitated, looking toward it. Maybe they'd moved on. The fire was out and she couldn't see anyone hanging around. What she'd thought was just a pile of sleeping bags, moved. "Well, someone's here," she said to herself.

She looked all around before getting out of her car, worried about the absence of Mama's group. Seeing no one, she got out. But she froze, thinking, *Maybe the person over there isn't even one of them.* Kaylee's mind flashed back to the man who'd attacked her the first night she'd found the group. Her chest seized, and she froze. Not taking her eyes off of the pile of sleeping bags, she reached blindly for her door handle.

A horrible, wet, barking cough brought her out of her fear induced shutdown. "Mama C!" She rushed over, keys still jangling in her hand.

The gravel scraped at Kaylee's knees as she slid to the ground beside Mama C. She pulled the covers back and gasped. Mama's lips were blue, her eyes nearly glazed over. Kaylee felt her forehead and jerked her hand away. She was burning up with fever.

"Mama C. Say something. It's Kaylee." Tears ran down her cheeks.

"Kaylee." The older woman's chest rattled as she worked to draw in a breath. Another fit of coughing took what little air she'd been able to get.

"Mama." Kaylee pulled at the sleeping bags and blankets, trying to get some cool air to Mama C's skin. "Where is everyone?"

Mama looked confused, tilting her head and scowling. "Don't know."

She needed to get to a hospital. Kaylee reached into her pocket before realizing she didn't have her phone. "Dammit!" She couldn't pull her car any closer and there was no way she'd be able to get Mama all the way over to it.

"Mama, I'll be right back."

She ran to her car, spun the wheels in the gravel, and sped to the nearest gas station where she called an ambulance to meet her back at the viaduct. Before rushing back to Mama C, she turned the flashers on so the ambulance would know they were in the right place.

Kaylee looked around for a bottle of water, but found only empty ones. Where were the others? Why was Mama C alone? Kaylee shivered in the dark as she waited for the ambulance. She kept one hand on the old woman's chest, worried that each next breath would be her last.

Finally, after what seemed like hours, the ambulance pulled up next to Kaylee's car. She met the paramedics halfway to where Mama C lay. "She's over there. Hurry." She led them to her.

They asked Kaylee a bunch of questions about Mama C's illness, her name, any family? Medical history? Kaylee answered what she could then asked, as they buckled Mama onto the stretcher, ready to put her in the back of the ambulance, "Where are you taking her?"

"Denver Health, over in Lincoln Park area. Are you coming with her?" the medic asked.

"Yes." She needed to tell Blayne. "I need to go tell my...her friend first. I'll go straight to the hospital after."

"Okay. You might want to hurry, she doesn't look so good. Who knows how long her oxygen sats have been in the sixties." They lifted her into the ambulance and sped away.

Kaylee rubbed her hands across her face and gulped air into her lungs. She had to calm down before telling Blayne. She got in her car, hoping he would be clear-headed when she got there. Hell, hoping he would be home.

CHAPTER 22

The car skidded to a halt and Kaylee looked up at the darkened windows of Blayne's apartment. *Maybe he just went to bed early.* She rummaged in her backpack for a pen and piece of paper so she could leave him a note if he didn't answer.

Stumbling up the stairs in her hurry, she skinned the palms of her hands on the metal steps. She pounded on the door and bit her nails as she waited. No answer. She pounded louder. Still no answer. Kaylee propped the paper up against the door to write a note.

Blayne – Mama C

Footsteps crunched on the gravel below.

"Well, look who we have here."

Kaylee dropped the pen, and the paper fluttered to the landing. Her heart raced. She gripped her keys so tight they dug into her hand. The guy Blayne had been arguing with the other day bounded up the stairs toward her, a sinister smile twisting his face. Kaylee turned and pounded on Blayne's door, she had nowhere to go.

The man grabbed her from behind, one arm around her waist, the other covering her mouth. He dragged her toward the stairs backwards. She kicked, and flailed her arms at his face. His hand covering her mouth slipped a little, and she sunk her teeth into it.

Swearing, he stepped to the side and flung her down the rest of the stairs. Her left shoulder hit first, followed by her head. She landed in a throbbing heap at the bottom, her mind too fuzzy to even attempt to get away.

Slow, deliberate steps thumped toward her. "You shouldn't 'a done that. We coulda done this the easy way."

Kaylee blinked up at him. He had her keys, swinging them around his finger. She pushed up to a half-sitting position, but a surge of dizziness and intense pain in her shoulder immobilized her. She dropped back down with a cry.

"Let me help you to your car, sweetheart. Don't worry, I'll drive. You're in no condition to man the wheel." He laughed then spit right next to her head.

He grabbed her under the arms and lifted. Her shoulder came alive with pain, like a dull wooden stake had been pounded through it. Her vision faded around the edges and she groaned. As he dragged her, the pain intensified to the point where everything went blissfully black.

HER WHOLE BODY ACHED. Every nerve ending screamed at Kaylee to slip back into unconscious oblivion. But she needed to stay awake. To think. She opened her eyes just a slit, taking in her surroundings. Her car. She laid across the back seat of her car, tires rolling beneath her. Before she could even begin to form a plan, the car came to a stop.

"We're heeere." Her kidnapper's voice raked across her brain like a dentist's drill boring into a raw nerve.

Should she pretend she was still out? The decision was made for her when he opened the rear door and started to pull her out by her arms again. "No!" she cried. "Let me. I'll do it myself. Let me do it myself."

The kidnapper stepped back and gestured for her to go ahead.

Kaylee held her breath and, clutching her left arm across her torso, she pulled herself up with her right, wincing at the sharp pain in her left shoulder.

"Hurry it up. We don't have all night." He snorted. "Just kidding. We have *all* the time in the world." His voice dripped with slime and Kaylee's stomach heaved.

Each movement sent a jolt of pain into her shoulder, but it was tolerable as long as she kept her arm pressed tight to her body. She scooted along the seat then stood on the cracked asphalt. Her sore left shoulder sagged lower than the right. She pushed aside the thoughts of what this snake wanted from her and concentrated on her surroundings. The outline of an enormous bowling pin peeking above the dark building made a shadow against the light of the moon. The distant sound of cars and lack of lighting nearby indicated the abandoned building was secluded. He'd parked at the back of the building—her car wouldn't even be visible from the deserted road.

"Come on, sweetheart." He yanked on her injured arm and she stifled a whimper.

She held her left arm with her right and wrenched away from him. "Don't touch me. I'll follow you."

He grabbed her face and jerked it toward him. "Oh, sweetheart, I'm going to touch you. You can bet on that." He looked her up and down and licked his lips.

Revulsion ran through her like flushing a toilet. Icy fingers of fear crept up her spine, and she shook her head, unable to speak.

"Let's get inside so I can show you what I mean." He winked and grabbed her arm again, pulling her toward the deserted bowling alley.

The metal door flew open before they reached it. "Carl," a man's shape was silhouetted against a dim light from inside, "what in the hell are you doing?"

Carl pushed Kaylee toward the door and the other man stepped back to avoid her. "I got Blayne's lady friend."

"What? Why?" A calculating smile spread across his face. "Ahh. Smart move. Let's get her inside."

There were no windows in the back of the building to reveal the light from the battery-operated lanterns sitting about. "Put her over there," the new guy pointed to a hard plastic chair, "and tie her up. I don't want her sneaking out when we aren't looking. We have product to cut and package."

"Dude," Carl plead, "I wanted to have some fun with her first. Take her to the office." He gestured to a door with a leering grin.

"Are you crazy? We want Blayne to work for us not kill us. Do what I said. And don't call me 'dude'."

"Gah, Aaron, you spoiled my fun."

"Just shut your mouth and get her tied up. We need to get a move on."

Carl shoved her none-too-gently into the chair. She drew a sharp breath and grit her teeth. She couldn't help but cry out when he grabbed her injured arm and yanked it to the armrest of the chair.

Aaron sauntered over. "What'd you do to her?" He leaned in closer, holding a lantern up. "She's all beat up!"

"I didn't do nothin'. She fell down the stairs."

"Yeah." Aaron pressed on her shoulder. Kaylee squeezed her eyes shut and tried to swallow the groan forcing its way out of her throat. "Her shoulder's dislocated." He looked at Carl. "Idiot. Let her put her arm the way she had it and just tie the rope around her and the chair. You can tie her other arm to the armrest. Leave her feet, she ain't going nowhere." As he walked away, Kaylee spotted the grip of a gun sticking out of the back of his jeans.

Carl muttered under his breath as he wrapped a long cord around her several times, pinning her left arm to her torso. He glanced in the direction Aaron had gone, then leered back at Kaylee, pausing in his duties to grope her. She raked her ragged fingernails across his face with her still-free right hand. He backhanded her, jarring her already concussed head. She refused the tears forming in her eyes, closing them tight as Carl tied her free hand to the chair.

His stinking breath stung her nostrils as he leaned close. Her eyes flew open as he gripped her face so tight her cheeks nearly touched. "That's the second time today you've drawn blood on me. You owe me somethin' for that." He slammed his mouth against hers, forcing his tongue inside.

Kaylee tried to pull away from him, twisting her head from side to side, but his fingernails dug into her cheeks, holding her face hostage. Her muffled protests only seemed to excite him more. Her stomach heaved, her throat constricting in a loud gag.

Carl reeled away from her, but still held fast to her face. "If you puke on me, I swear—"

"Carl!" Aaron yelled from an unseen doorway. "Get in here and help me! How long does it take to tie someone up?"

With one more rough grope, Carl whispered, "Aaron won't always be around." He walked away, his footsteps echoing on the tile floor.

Kaylee struggled against her bindings, but they were too tight, and her head was pounding, her shoulder aching. She gave up and gave in to the infuriating tears. Her breath hitched as the tears flowed freely. How had this happened? Where was Blayne? *Damn him!*

CHAPTER 23

Loud voices awakened Kaylee from her uncomfortable sleep. She lifted her head, wincing at the pain in her neck, and shoulder, and, well, everywhere. She had no idea what time of day or night it was.

"Dammit, Carl! Now she has bruises on her face. Blayne's gonna' freak." Aaron and the object of his ire stood a few paces off.

"Come on, dude. It'll just make him more likely to cooperate with us."

Aaron glanced at Kaylee then back at Carl. "Maybe. Where'd you put her phone? Let's get this over with, we have a ton of product to move."

Carl dug in his pocket and handed him Kaylee's phone.

"Where did you get that?" she asked.

"You dropped it." Carl smirked. "And finders keepers."

No wonder Allie hadn't been able to find it when she'd gone to look.

"Your boyfriend's been texting and calling non-stop for the past few days. Too bad we couldn't figure out your code so we could mess with him a little."

"Speaking of code," Aaron said, "what is it?"

Blayne had been trying to get ahold of her. Why hadn't he just come to her apartment?

Aaron snapped in her face. "The code, princess."

"Why should I tell you?" She lifted her chin in defiance.

He leaned in close to her face. "Because us getting ahold of Blayne is your only ticket out of here."

"Use your own phone." Her wobbly voice gave away her fake bravado.

"Listen, princess, he'll answer if he thinks it's you. Now, I'm only going to ask one more time and then I'm gonna let Carl have his way with you if you refuse again—what's the code?"

Kaylee glanced at Carl and swallowed. "Two, nine, four, six."

He patted her on the arm. "Good girl." He stood and jabbed at the screen of her phone. "Here are the rules. They're simple. I'm going to talk to your boyfriend and you are going to keep quiet. One peep from you, and, again, Carl."

Carl mimed an obscene gesture as he leered at her.

Kaylee looked away from him and nodded.

Aaron thumbed through what she assumed were her text messages. "Wow. Blayne has it bad for you. 'I'm so sorry.' 'Let me explain.' 'Kaylee please.' 'Please just answer me so I know you're okay.'" He rolled his eyes and laughed. "Who knew Blayne was so fragile? Let's see what his voice messages say, shall we?"

"No!" Kaylee fought against her restraints. "That's none of your business!"

He ignored her and put it on speaker-phone. "*Kaylee, I'm so sorry. Please just call me back, I can explain.*"

"Oh," Aaron said mockingly, "he sounds so *upset*."

"There are just too many to listen to all of them, let's skip to the end." Blayne's voice sounded distant and hoarse. "*Kaylee, I won't bother you again. It's obvious that you don't want to talk to me. But I still want to explain. That guy I was talking to was from my old life. He's dangerous and his friends are dangerous and I didn't want him to know you're someone I care about. They wanted me to sell drugs for them again, but I said no. I'm done with that life, for good. You're the best thing that's ever happened to me. I hope I see you around sometime.*" His voice hitched on the last word, and it broke Kaylee's heart.

He sounded so defeated. She was so stupid! Why had she ever doubted him? Hot tears spilled from her eyes.

"See, even your boyfriend knows we're dangerous. Now remember," Aaron said, "not a sound from you." He pushed against her injured shoulder for emphasis.

He moved away from her and put the phone to his ear, his back toward her. "Well, hello there, Blayne. Sorry to disappoint you, you sounded so excited, but this isn't Kaylee."

He paused and listened for a second.

"Good job. I'm so flattered that you recognized my voice."

Another pause.

"No need for name-calling. She's right here, wanna see?" Aaron turned to her, Carl looking on with a grin. "Remember the rules, princess." He switched it to speaker and hit the Facetime icon, holding the phone up in front of him as he turned his back again, the camera capturing Kaylee in the background.

"Wave to your boyfriend, princess." He and Carl laughed. "Oh, wait, you can't. You're all tied up at the moment."

"Aaron," Kaylee had never heard Blayne sound so furious before. "I will kill you."

"Now Blayne, I think we can reach a non-homicidal solution here."

"Let me see her close up!"

"Now hold on," Aaron said. "I believe I hold all the cards here and I'm not done speaking."

Kaylee could see the murderous rage in Blayne's eyes from several feet away. Seeing him made her cry even harder.

An inhuman roar rose from the depths of Blayne's bowels and he ripped at his hair with his free hand, his camera shaking around violently.

"Calm down, man." A touch of fear sounded in Aaron's voice. Carl even backed away from the phone like Blayne would come lunging through it at any minute. "Look, we just wanted to get your attention. The chick is fine, see?" He backed up closer to her and tilted the phone so the camera captured more of her face than his.

Hoping that Aaron's attention was solely on the rage-filled

Blayne, Kaylee mouthed the words, "*Bowling alley. I'm at a deserted bowling alley.*"

"Let me see just her, up close." Blayne's voice had changed slightly. Had he seen her attempt to communicate with him? "Now!"

Aaron jumped then tried to cover it up with a laugh. "Fine, but then we negotiate."

He shoved the phone close to her face.

"Kaylee," he breathed. "Are you okay?"

She glanced at Aaron then back at the phone. She nodded.

"She ain't allowed to talk," Carl yelled from behind Aaron.

Blayne's eyes narrowed. Anger and frustration painted lines on his forehead. He signed: *I'm coming.* Kaylee shook her head, her eyes widening with the fear running rampant inside her. Fear for him, not for herself. *They have guns!* She wanted to yell. She bit her lips and cried harder, audible sobs erupting from her throat now as she shook her head harder.

Blayne pleaded, "I'm sorry, Kaylee. I'm so sorry you got brought into this mess." He swiped an angry tear from his cheek.

Aaron pulled the phone back to his own face. "Enough. You seen that she's fine—"

"Fine?" Blayne interrupted. "She is not fine! She has bruises and scrapes all over her face!"

"Well, she ain't dead yet." Aaron's voice deepened ominously.

"What do you want?" Blayne asked.

Aaron turned off the Facetime but left it on speaker. "I just want you to come back to the fold, brother. You were our best dealer before that old hag got ahold of ya. Just help us unload this shipment. The cartel gave us three days and we know you can do it in two."

"And what about Kaylee?"

"Oh, we'll keep her here with us until it's done. Insurance. Carl will take good care of her."

"Don't you let that bastard anywhere near her!"

"Hey! I thought we were friends." Carl laughed.

"Okay, okay," Aaron said. "I'll send *him* to you with the product, and *I'll* stay here with the princess. Do we have a deal?"

Blayne growled. "Yeah. We have a deal. When and where will Carl make the drop?"

"No!" Kaylee shouted.

Aaron backhanded her. "I told you to stay quiet!"

The quiet, low rumble of Blayne's voice was more terrifying than any outburst Kaylee had ever heard. "Touch her again, and I will skin you alive and feed your own flesh to you."

Blood trickled down her chin from a cut on her lip. She was glad the camera was off. She didn't want Blayne to endanger himself for her.

"Sorry," Aaron mumbled. "I won't touch her. Sorry, man." He ran a hand through his hair. "Meet Carl tonight at ten at the old drop off."

"Blayne..." Kaylee wanted to tell him about Mama C. Maybe that would keep him away, convince him to just call the police to find her.

Aaron ended the call and stepped up close to her. "I told you to shut up." He slapped her again.

Kaylee narrowed her eyes and spit in his face.

A bloody glob of spit dripped from the corner of his mouth. He raised his hand again, but Carl grabbed it. "We got what we want, dude. Let's not make Blayne any madder."

Aaron jerked his arm out of Carl's grasp. "Fine. Let's get it all sorted and packed into the bags. We have three hours before the drop off."

Kaylee had to think of a way to escape before then. The low-life men walked toward the closed door where she assumed they kept the drugs. "Wait," she said. "I need to go to the bathroom."

"I'll take her," Carl quickly volunteered with a leering smile.

"No," Aaron shoved him toward the door. "You get started and I'll take her."

He pulled out a large pocket knife and cut the ropes near the knots Carl had tied. He untwisted the ropes from around her and then pulled her up by her right arm. She wavered, her head swam and her feet tingled. She unwillingly leaned into her captor rather than fall to the ground.

"I just need a second. Dizzy," she said.

"I don't have all day. Let's go." He pushed her toward the front of the building. "Bathrooms are up front."

He held to her with one hand and clutched the lantern with the other. He stopped outside the women's bathroom and handed her the lantern. "I'll wait out here. But if you take too long or try anything funny, I'm coming in."

Kaylee's heart dropped as she entered. No windows. Not that she would have been able to climb out with her arm hanging useless from its socket. She struggled to unbutton her pants one-handed, but managed, trying to think as she sat on the disgusting toilet. Maybe she could make a run for it, find a way out through the front of the building. "Hey! Can you get me some toilet paper?" she yelled.

"No! You can drip dry," Aaron replied.

She would have to think of a way to escape before Blayne charged in. She rested her forehead in her hand, rocking back and forth.

"You have thirty seconds to get out here or I'm coming in!" Aaron yelled.

She stood, wobbling a little, and pulled her pants up with one hand. She struggled to button them, finally using her injured arm with a gasp of pain. There was no way she'd go back out there with her pants unbuttoned.

Shoulder screaming with pain, she met Aaron at the entrance just as he stepped inside with a growl.

"Come on. I have stuff to do." He started walking, leaving her to follow behind.

Kaylee glanced around, hoping to find an opening she could get through to the outside. Everything appeared to be boarded up. She sighed then looked back at Aaron as she stepped to follow him. *The gun.* She could barely make it out in the dim light, but it was still there, stuck in the waistband of his pants. She quickened her steps, waiting until she was right behind him before making her move. They'd made it almost to the doorway into the back when she reached for it. Wrapping her fingers around the grip, she stopped and backed up a few steps. Relying on training from trips to the gun range with her father, she clicked off the safety and aimed the gun at Aaron's back with a shaking hand. "Turn around."

He turned slowly, raising his hands up to the height of his shoulders. "Now, princess. That wasn't very nice." He nodded to the gun. "Too bad there isn't a bullet in the chamber, no way you can chamber one, what with an injured shoulder and all." He shook his head.

She called his bluff. "I don't believe you. Someone like you wouldn't go around with an unchambered pistol. Plus, the safety was on, no need for that unless it was ready to fire." She could see by the falter in his smile that she'd guessed correctly.

His face twisted into an angry snarl. "What are you going to do now, princess? Shoot me?"

"Only if you make me." Again, the trembling in her voice betrayed her. "Just give me my car keys and phone, and I'll be out of your hair."

"No deal. You'll have to shoot me."

She tightened her grip and moved it to aim square at his chest. "Have it your way." Kaylee didn't think she could do it, but she wanted him to believe she would.

Eyes widening, Aaron stepped back. "Wait—"

A noise behind her caused Kaylee to turn. Carl. He pushed her gun hand up toward the ceiling and punched her in the kidney with his other fist. Pain sliced into her, stealing her breath as she buckled over. Every muscle tensed, including her trigger finger, and she shot into the ceiling. Carl grabbed her wrist and twisted it painfully. The gun dropped to the floor.

"You'd better hope nobody heard that gunshot, princess." Aaron grabbed her arm and dragged her back to the chair. He retied the cords around her tighter than before. "If you need to pee again, you'll do it in your pants."

The drug-dealing kidnappers disappeared behind the door to the drug room. Kaylee couldn't even struggle to loosen the cords. Every inch of her body ached and all she could do was cry until she had no more tears and hope that Blayne would call the police instead of coming for her himself.

CHAPTER 24

Shivering in the dilapidated building, Kaylee was surrounded by darkness and pain. She had no idea how long it had been since the phone call as every minute seemed to drag on for hours. She had strongly considered asking the kidnappers for some of their drugs to dull the pain, but she knew she wouldn't. She didn't want to go down that road.

After what seemed like days, Aaron and Carl came out of the drug room, each carrying a duffle bag. *Just like in the movies*, Kaylee thought, squinting as the light from the lantern hit her eyes.

Aaron shined the light closer to her battered face. "Man, Blayne is going to kill us when he sees this."

"Yeah." Carl's face turned ashen and his voice came out in a higher pitch than normal. "Maybe we should just kill him after he sells this stuff off."

"No!" Kaylee shouted. "You have a deal. I'll make sure he doesn't come after you. Please."

The color somewhat returned to Carl's face, along with a twitchy smile. "I could keep you, then. As a prize."

"Knock it off, Carl," Aaron said. "We ain't gonna kill Blayne."

Kaylee was not comforted by his words. These guys were scum. They couldn't be trusted to keep their word.

Aaron shoved his bag at Carl. "You'd better get going. You'll wanna get there before him, scope things out."

Carl grabbed the bag. "You sure you don't wanna let me stay here?" He glanced at Kaylee and licked his lips.

"Get going." Aaron kicked him in the butt, pushing him toward the exit.

When he'd left, Aaron turned to her. "Let's see about getting you cleaned up. It'll be a couple days before Blayne can cash in on the product, maybe I can get rid of some of the physical evidence on your face before then." He was talking to himself more than her. She didn't even bother to answer.

He looked at her and tilted his head. "You thirsty? You probably are. I'll get you some water, too." He walked through the door leading to the front of the building, letting it close behind him.

Kaylee was facing away from the back door, but she heard it slide open softly. Her heart sped up. Was Carl back? Why would he be back already?

Quiet footsteps padded toward her. It couldn't have been Carl, the footfalls were too soft. Carl clodded around like a cow. Then—his scent hit her. Her chest squeezed in on itself. "Blayne," she whispered. "No."

"Shh. It's okay." The beam from his flashlight splayed out before them. He knelt behind her, working at the knots of her bindings.

Fear formed a lump in her throat. She choked out, "You have to leave. Aaron's here. He has a gun."

Blayne stopped messing with the cord and stepped in front of her, careful not to shine the light directly in her eyes. "Where is he?" he whispered. Then, catching sight of her banged up face, his eyes turned cold, and he ground his teeth. "I'm going to kill him."

"No. Blayne. Please," she begged. "Just leave and call the police. Please."

"Where is he?" he asked again.

"He'll be back any minute." Her eyes gave her away as she glanced at the door to the front.

Blayne's face softened a fraction, and he stroked her tangled mess of hair. He leaned down and kissed her forehead with more gentleness than the touch of a feather. "It'll be okay." He stopped after taking several steps and turned back to her. "I love you, Kaylee."

Her next breath came as a sob. Her body trembled with fear and pain and shock as Blayne walked toward the door. He clicked the flashlight off as he got closer, then crouched to the side of the door, waiting.

Kaylee had trouble breathing. She couldn't seem to get enough air. Her lips went numb. Her fingers tingled. She knew she was hyperventilating but couldn't stop herself. Blayne loved her—and he was now risking his life for her.

Aaron's heavy boots stomped on the other side of the door. He opened it, Blayne still poised behind it. "I got ya some water, princess. And a wet rag so I can clean ya up a little before Blayne—"

Blayne slammed the door into Aaron, pinning him between it and the doorjamb. Aaron cried out in pain and dropped the water.

"Before Blayne *what*?" Blayne growled.

Half the kidnapper's body and all of his head were on this side of the door. He grunted and breathed in short snaps of breath as Blayne put more pressure on his chest with the door. "You. Blayne. Carl. He'll be back when you don't show. Any minute."

"Don't worry about Carl. I made sure someone was there to meet him." Blayne sneered. "He won't be back."

Aaron's eyes widened and his face turned the color of a plum. He shifted, trying to get out of the door, it seemed. A loud blast filled the air and echoed in the near empty building. Blayne flew back from the door and Kaylee screamed as it swung back, slamming into the wall—a hole piercing the metal at the height of Blayne's chest.

Her whole body numb, Kaylee fought her restraints. "No! Blayne!" The chair jumped and rattled against the hard floor.

Aaron put his hands on his knees, gulping in lungfuls of air. He edged over, gun pointed out in front of him, to where Blayne lay unmoving on the ground.

Kaylee rocked the chair side to side, pushing it with her feet.

Aaron leaned over Blayne's body, still pointing the gun at him.

The chair tipped, jarring Kaylee's already busted up body. The armrest where her right arm was tied shattered, as did the part of the back of the chair that hit the ground. She shimmied out of her bonds, holding her left arm close to her body.

Aaron whipped around at the noise, and Blayne shot a leg out, sweeping the gun from Aaron's hand. Aaron lunged for it, but Blayne caught one of his ankles as he twisted up and around. Aaron fell, tripped up by Blayne's grasp, and Blayne cried out with pain. Blood stained his shirt from a wound near his left collar bone.

Kaylee, teeth clenched against the scream in her throat, crawled toward the gun. Aaron coiled around and pounded on Blayne's hand. The veins in Blayne's neck bulged as he pulled Aaron toward him.

The gun lay just inches away from Kaylee's reach. Aaron threw himself toward it, kicking at Blayne's grasp on his ankle. They reached it at the same time, but Aaron wrenched it from her fingers and clouted her on the side of the head with it then turned it on Blayne. She fought through the dizziness and screamed her rage as she lurched to her feet toward him. She kicked at his face, a weak but effective gesture that threw off his aim. The bullet ricocheted off the cement floor next to Blayne's face.

Blayne roared and sprang to his knees. He grabbed Aaron's wrist and wrenched it back with a loud crack. The drug dealer dropped the gun with a squeal of pain. Kaylee picked it up, pointing it at her captor. She caught movement out of the corner of her eye as Blayne pounded his fist into Aaron's jaw, knocking him to the ground. With a grunt, Blayne straddled him, hammering his fist into Aaron's face over and over until his nose was an unrecognizable blob of blood and tissue pressed flat against his face.

"Blayne. Blayne stop!" Kaylee knelt beside him.

Blayne stopped mid-punch and looked at her. His face drained of color as all his adrenaline fled in a rush. He slumped to the floor next to Aaron.

"Blayne, no!" Kaylee dropped the gun and struggled to turn him on his back with one arm. He groaned—and her frozen heart started beating again at the sound of life. He rolled over, his shirt now drenched in blood, his own and Aaron's. Kaylee pressed her hand to his wound to stop the bleeding.

"Ouch," he mumbled. He raised his tremulous right hand to her face and touched her cheek before letting it drop.

"Blayne, just hold on, okay. Just hold on." She needed to find a phone. Her eyes searched his pockets, but she didn't want to remove the pressure from his wound.

Sirens echoed in the distance. Kaylee cocked her head. Were they coming closer? She leaned in next to Blayne's ear. "Hang on. Help is coming." Her tears fell on his face as she brushed her lips against his. "Please, Blayne, look at me. Stay with me."

He grunted and opened his eyes with apparent effort.

"I love you, too," she whispered. "Do you hear me? I love you, too."

His pale lips curved into a feeble smile.

The sirens grew louder and cars screeched to a stop outside the bowling alley.

CHAPTER 25

Beeping. What was that beeping sound? Kaylee opened her eyes with effort, it felt like a ten-pound weight was attached to each eyelid. Her mouth felt like she'd been sucking on cotton balls. Bright light stung her eyes, making her blink.

"Miss Burke? Glad to see you're waking up. My name is Denise, how are you feeling?"

Kaylee focused on the nurse at her bedside and the events that brought her there flooded her mind. "Blayne. How's Blayne?" She tried to sit up but found she couldn't use her left arm. Looking down, she saw that it was in a sling with a band wrapped around her arm and body, keeping it from moving. Her shoulder had been dislocated, and they'd sedated her to put it back in place.

"Mr. Ellis is still in surgery," Denise smiled sadly. "I'm afraid that's all I can tell you."

Kaylee nodded. She knew all about HIPAA, it's why Max couldn't tell them all the cool stuff he saw at the hospital. "Can I see him when he gets out of recovery?" She wouldn't even consider the idea that he wouldn't make it.

The nurse nodded. "As long as he consents. I'm going to sit you up and give you some water. You've gotten two liters of IV fluids because of your extreme dehydration, but we need to make sure you can hold down liquids, and then some real food." She pushed a button on the side of the bed that raised Kaylee to a semi-sitting position.

"Okay." It had been well over twenty-four hours since she'd last eaten or drunk anything, yet she had zero appetite. Her worry about Blayne took care of that.

Denise headed toward the curtain, but before she reached it, another thought struck Kaylee and she blurted out, "Mama C."

The nurse turned back to her, forehead scrunched in confusion. "What?"

"Mama C. Before I got taken, I called an ambulance to have a friend, Claire Watson, brought in." She was afraid to ask the next question. She swallowed. "Can you please check on her? And let me know if she's alive?"

That sad smile touched the nurse's face again. "I will. I'll be back in just a minute."

Kaylee laid her head back and closed her eyes, allowing a tear to trickle down her face.

Denise returned with a Styrofoam cup of ice water and a straw. Kaylee took it from her and took a few sips. The cold water felt good on her parched mouth. "Did you find out anything?"

Taking the cup from her, Denise said, "Mrs. Watson is alive. But she isn't doing well. Do you know if she has any family?"

As much as Kaylee wanted to press the nurse for more information, she knew Denise wouldn't be able to tell her more. She shook her head. "She has no one. Well, no living relatives. She does have a family though, just not one made with blood."

"Unfortunately, that doesn't count in the eyes of the law." She glanced at the curtain as it parted. "It looks like Dr. Ekins is here to let you know the plan."

"Hi Kaylee, I'm Dr. Ekins, or Lisa if you prefer. The shoulder reduction went well. I was a little worried that it would be difficult because of the extended amount of time it was dislocated. We're going to leave it in a sling and swath for several weeks, keep icing it for the next two days, and have you follow up with an Orthopedic doctor."

"When can I be discharged?" Kaylee asked, anxious to go visit Mama C.

"Well," the doctor said, "if it were just your shoulder injury we had to worry about, I'd let you go as soon as we make sure you can hold down some fluids. But you've also had a pretty serious head injury. So, the plan is to move you out of the ER and admit you to the neuro unit so they can monitor you for the next twenty-four hours."

Kaylee frowned. "Will I be able to visit another patient while I'm admitted?" *Two other patients,* she thought.

"That will be up to the attending on neuro, but I don't see why not." Dr. Ekins laid her hand on Kaylee's arm, warmth radiated from the doctor's face and touch. "You've been through quite a lot, Kaylee. I can see that you're a strong woman." She paused. "But please give yourself some time to heal. Not just physically, but mentally and emotionally as well. Be kind to yourself when you have a bad moment or a bad day in the coming weeks. Allow yourself to cry if you need to. Lean on your friends—one of which is in the waiting room, eager to see you."

Kaylee perked up. "Allie?"

Dr. Ekins nodded. "I'll send her in now, and she can follow you down to the floor when the nurses are ready."

A few minutes later, Allie rushed in and hugged Kaylee awkwardly around the IV tubing and monitors. "Kaylee! I'm so glad you're okay."

"How did you know I was here?"

"That amazing boyfriend of yours." Allie smiled.

"What? But he's in surgery, he was in critical condition when we got here."

Allie shook her head. "No, I knew you were kidnapped. He came to the apartment after they called him. He was freaking out, he was so worried about you. And I've never seen anyone so angry."

Kaylee was so confused. "Why did he come to the apartment?"

"He videoed part of the Facetime. That was genius of you to mouth where you were, but he wasn't a hundred percent positive what you'd said, so he brought it to show me. He called the police to give them an anonymous tip about the drug meet-up."

Kaylee interrupted. "That's what he meant..."

"Then he insisted on borrowing my car and took off in a frenzy," Allie continued. "He texted me, I assume when he got to the bowling alley, and told me to call the police in ten minutes and tell them to go there."

Grasping her friend's hand, Kaylee said, "Thank you."

Allie wiped at her face, as she was now crying. "Of course, Kay, I'd do anything for you. And obviously, so would Blayne. The police let me know you were on your way here in an ambulance."

"I'm glad you're here." Kaylee squeezed her friend's hand.

"Oh, and,"—Allie winced—"I called your parents. They're on their way up here."

The neuro attending didn't want Kaylee to leave her room until he'd had a chance to reassess her later in the day. But her nurse and Allie conspired against him as soon as they got word that Blayne was out of the recovery room and in the med/surg unit on the same floor as neuro.

"You're my only patient right now," said Tammy, the nurse assigned to her. "So, I'll just go with you. I can do your neuro checks on the go." She winked.

The dread Kaylee had been feeling since Blayne had been closed into the back of an ambulance eased somewhat. Tammy had assured her that he must be doing fine, or they wouldn't have put him on med/surg, he would be in the surgical ICU.

They'd already unhooked her from the IV fluids, leaving the capped IV in Kaylee's arm. She grew dizzy when transferring to the wheelchair Tammy insisted on using, but she didn't tell the nurse about it. She didn't want anything to keep her from Blayne.

The nurse pushed her into his room, Allie close behind them. Blayne lay in bed, the head of the bed slightly elevated, an identical sling to hers on his left arm. His face was still pale, but not the deathly white it had been the last time she'd seen him. He smiled and reached out to her as Tammy wheeled her right next to him. "Kaylee," he clutched her hand. "I'm so sorry."

His name came from her mouth as a sob. "Blayne." She stood shakily from the wheelchair and laid her head against his chest, taking the ER doctor's advice and allowing herself to lose control and weep. With some trouble and some help by Tammy to untangle his IV tubing, Blayne hugged her to his chest with his uninjured arm. He pressed his lips to her head, holding them there as she let hot tears flow onto his hospital gown.

In the background, she heard Tammy whisper, "Let's give them some privacy," and shortly after, the door opened and closed.

Blayne just held her without saying a word until she'd let it all out. The pent-up fear, the flood of relief that he was alive, the worry about Mama C. After several minutes, she pulled herself together, sat back in the wheelchair, and wiped her face. She realized at that moment what she must look like—dirty, tangled hair; no makeup; hospital gown. But she didn't care.

They held hands, Kaylee ran her thumb across Blayne's red, swollen knuckles. He repeated, "I'm so sorry—"

"Don't," Kaylee said. "Don't apologize. None of this is your fault."

"If I hadn't been such an idiot in my past—"

"No. Stop," she commanded with a soft voice. "This is a new day. And you can't control what other people think and do. It wasn't your fault."

He looked up at the ceiling and pursed his lips. He whispered, "I was so afraid I was going to lose you." He closed his eyes and swallowed, then looked at her again. "I've never been so scared in my life. Or so angry." He shook his head and let go of her hand. He softly ran his fingers over her bruised face, her swollen lip, the worry lines creasing her forehead. He fixed her gaze with his eyes. "I love you, Kaylee. I wanted to tell you. I started to tell you a couple of times and I didn't. Then I was afraid I'd lost the chance. When you wouldn't answer your phone or texts, then when those assholes had you. That's why I said it at the bowling alley, just in case." He grabbed her hand. "I will never again pass up the opportunity to tell you how much you mean to me. Ever."

"I love you, too. And thank you. For saving my life." She narrowed her eyes at him. "But don't you ever risk your life like that again."

He smiled wearily. "No guarantees." He lifted her hand to his lips and kissed it, his lips lingering there, flushing her skin with warmth. He held it there even as the door opened and Allie, Tammy, and a doctor entered, only returning their hands to the bed when the doctor stood next to him.

"Well Mr. Ellis, you were quite lucky. I'm Dr. Bennet. I'm the surgeon who operated on you." He unsnapped Blayne's gown over his left shoulder and rolled it down to look at the dressing. "Now that you're more awake, I'll explain what I did.

"The bullet missed your subclavian artery by about five millimeters. Had it punctured that artery, you would have bled out in minutes. As it was, you were minutes away from dying due to blood loss without the artery being damaged. We transfused two units of blood. I removed the bullet and repaired your shattered clavicle using a few metal plates and screws. I project that you'll regain full function of your arm and shoulder barring any unseen nerve damage."

Dr. Bennet reached over and pressed on Blayne's left hand. "Can you feel that?"

Blayne nodded.

"Wiggle your fingers for me."

Blayne complied.

The doctor nodded. "You're getting antibiotics now. As per your request as we wheeled you into the operating room, you've been given no narcotics. Your surgical site should still be numb for a few more hours thanks to the nerve block, but it's going to be flaring with pain when that wears off. Are you still refusing narcotics?"

"Yes. I don't want any narcotics."

"Okay. I'll write an order for ketorolac, it's like a super ibuprofen, NSAID. That should take the edge off, at least. Do you have any questions for me?"

"When can I get out of here? And when can I go back to work?" Blayne asked.

"I anticipate that I'll be able to release you sometime tomorrow. As far as work goes, you will not be able to do any moderate to heavy labor or lifting for about six weeks. You'll be in that sling for about two weeks and probably need some physical therapy. Hopefully your work can accommodate that."

Blayne sighed. "I hope so."

After the doctor left the room, Tammy, Kaylee's nurse, said, "I'd better get you back to your room before the neuro team does their rounds."

"Okay," Kaylee said. "Thank you so much for bringing me down here. Can I have just a couple more minutes, please?"

Tammy smiled and nodded.

Allie patted Blayne's hand. "I guess you won't be signing to me for a few weeks. You're going to have to shave soon or I won't be able to read your lips, either." She bent over and kissed his cheek then whispered, "Thank you for saving my friend."

"Thank *you* for being there when we both needed you."

Allie winked at him then left the room with Tammy.

"I need to tell you something," Kaylee said.

"I don't like the way you said that." His voice trailed off, and his eyes closed for a bit longer than a normal blink.

"Well, the reason I was at your apartment was to tell you that Mama C... I went to check on her and she was worse. Much worse."

"Is she..." Panic rose in his voice.

"She's alive," Kaylee hurried to say. "But it doesn't look good. I called an ambulance. They brought her here, and I went straight to your house. I haven't seen her since then. She's in the ICU."

Blayne let go of her hand and grabbed the side rail to pull himself up. His face paled, and he fell back against the bed. "I need to see her."

"I know." She caressed his arm. "Get some rest first. It's too early in the morning to be visiting, anyway. We'll sneak down later."

"That's right," he mumbled, eyes closed. "I forgot it was practically the middle of the night."

Kaylee put her tired, achy muscles to work one more time to stand and brush his lips with hers. "I love you, Blayne," she whispered.

His lips twitched to a smile. "Love you, too. So much."

She brushed his hair back and stared at his sleeping face until Tammy came back in to take her back to her room.

CHAPTER 26

The rattling of Mama C's labored breaths filled the otherwise silent room. Kaylee gripped the door to steady herself. As soon as the neuro doctor had said she could get up and walk around, she'd headed to the MICU to see Mama C.

It was late afternoon. Allie had gone to her nursing clinicals and Blayne was sleeping when she'd peeked in on him.

A nurse stood at the bedside, trying to get Mama C to drink some water. "It looks like you have a visitor, Mrs. Watson." As the nurse slipped past Kaylee she whispered, "Try to get her to drink something."

Kaylee nodded and moved into the room. She leaned over Mama C so she could see into her eyes. "Mama. It's so good to see you."

The old woman's eyes widened. "What happened," she paused for breath, then continued, "to you?"

"Don't worry about me. I'm fine. I just took a tumble down some stairs." It wasn't a complete lie. "They tell me you aren't doing so great."

"It's my time to go, dear." She patted Kaylee's hand.

"No. No," said Kaylee. "There has to be more they can do than just give you oxygen!"

Mama C coughed then took several minutes to catch her breath before responding. "I don't want them to, Kaylee. You listen to me, okay?"

Kaylee nodded, fighting back tears.

"If my heart stops, don't you dare let 'em pound on my chest. You tell 'em just let me go be with my..." Another fit of coughing cut her off. It sounded like her lungs were full of gunk. An alarm started beeping, and the nurse came back in.

Kaylee looked at her questioningly.

"It's her oxygen. Every time she has one of these coughing spells, her O2 drops." She laid a hand on Mama C's arm and shook her head. "She's refusing to be intubated or even to have CPaP."

Mama's eyes pleaded with Kaylee. "I want to go be with my Daniel and Gene. I want to see my Savior."

"How can you believe in God after what has happened to you?" Kaylee spit out before thinking.

Mama C narrowed her eyes. "How do you know?"

"I dug a little into your past." Kaylee looked away from her.

"Nosy college girl."

Kaylee let out a sound that was half laugh/half cry. "How can you still believe?" she asked again.

Mama C grabbed her arm with a strength that belied her condition. "God is my only hope. He's the only way back to them."

"Mrs. Watson, you need to get some rest." The nurse looked at Kaylee. "Can I talk to you for a minute?"

Kaylee nodded but said to Mama C. "I'll be back later."

Mama C closed her eyes. "Bring Blayne."

Out in the hallway, the nurse said, "If she keeps refusing treatment, we're going to have to put her on hospice. Do you know what that is?"

Kaylee nodded. Her grandma had been on hospice. It was the care given to someone at the end of their life, when nothing else could be done. Or when the person didn't want anything else done to try to save them.

"Are you related to her?" the nurse asked.

"No. She doesn't have any living relatives."

"And, she's of a sound mind, no doubt about that. Stubborn woman." The nurse smiled wryly.

"That she is." Kaylee agreed. "I don't suppose you can force her to accept treatment?"

"Nope. She has the right to choose. Plus, I don't know that it would result in a good outcome, anyway. Sometimes medical treatment is just prolonging death, not life. Her lungs are shot. She also had a heart attack sometime in the last few days, so her heart isn't doing great either."

"Heart attack?" Kaylee cursed herself for not checking on Mama C sooner.

The nurse nodded and touched Kaylee's arm briefly. "I have to go get Mrs. Watson's breathing treatment and antibiotic set up. You can come back any time before eight o'clock tonight."

KAYLEE'S PARENTS waited for her back at her room, hurrying to her for an embrace as she walked in.

"Mom, you're hurting me."

Her mom released her hug and wiped at her tear strewn face. "I'm sorry, Kay. Are you okay?"

"I'm fine. You guys didn't have to drive all the way up here."

"Oh, yes we did, young lady." Her dad's stern voice made her smile.

Luke, her fifteen-year-old brother popped into the room carrying a soda. "Kaylee! What the heck, sister? Do I need to move up here with you to keep you out of trouble?" He gave her a one-armed hug.

Even though part of her heart was breaking over Mama C, a big part warmed up like a Christmas fire. She laughed. "I'm glad you're all here."

"The nurse came in while you were gone," her mom said. "She said they're going to discharge you in a couple of hours."

"Oh, good. I was afraid they'd make me stay until tomorrow." Kaylee sat on the bed.

"So," her dad said. "What exactly happened to you?"

"Yeah," Luke said. "Allie didn't tell us anything."

Kaylee sighed. She spent the next hour telling them everything. Well, almost everything.

DISCHARGE PAPERS IN HAND, Kaylee headed down to Blayne's room. Her family had gone to the cafeteria to get dinner and would text her on the new phone they'd brought her when they were done. She'd have to get the number switched to her old number, but she was thankful to have it. Who knew how long the police would hold on to hers for evidence? Looking at the settings on the phone reminded her she still needed to call Beth, Mama C's friend in New York. She hoped the number had automatically stored to the Cloud. She logged in and found it. Her heart raced as she dialed. How was she going to tell Beth that Mama C was just giving up, going on hospice?

"Hello?" the familiar voice answered.

"Hi, um, Beth?" Kaylee said.

"This is Beth." Her voice picked up a little as she said, "Is this Kaylee?"

"Yes."

"What in tarnation took you so long to call me, girl?"

"It's a long story—"

"Well, you can tell me about it later, let me talk to Claire."

"Well, I will let you talk to her later. I just wanted to call first to... to warn you."

"Warn me about what?" Beth asked.

"Mama...*Claire* is really sick. She's in the hospital and, well, she's giving up, Beth. She's refusing treatment. They want to put her on hospice." Kaylee's voice cracked.

"Oh no." Anguish dripped in Beth's voice. The anguish of someone who'd just found a long-lost friend only to be losing them again, for good.

"I'm so sorry, Beth." Kaylee wiped the moisture from her cheeks. "I'll let you talk to her when I go back to see her later."

SHE SLIPPED into Blayne's room, happy to see he was awake and sitting up eating Jell-O. Or trying to. He was having trouble negotiating with one hand.

"Need some help?" Kaylee asked.

His smile still looked exhausted, but his eyes lit up when he saw her. "Yes. Go get me a cheeseburger. This stuff stinks."

Kaylee raised an eyebrow at him. "You have to start out slow. Here," she reached for the Jell-O container, "let me help you. Between the two of us we have two good arms."

She held it while he spooned it out and mostly into his mouth. "Maybe they should get gowns the same color as their Jell-O." Kaylee wiped his chest with a napkin, the red stain not going anywhere.

"So," she said. "You're looking better than you did this morning."

"You too."

"It's amazing what a shower and hairbrush will do."

He ran his fingers through her hair, his intense gaze locked on hers.

"But, seriously," she said, a bit of hoarseness in her voice. "How are you feeling?"

"Seriously?" His arm dropped, and he leaned back against the pillow. "The nerve block is wearing off. And it hurts."

"Did they give you some of that medicine the doctor talked about?" Kaylee wrinkled her forehead.

"Not yet. I was going to try to tough it out."

Kaylee shook her head and pushed the button to signal the nurse.

A voice came over the little speaker on the side rail. "Can I help you?"

Blayne tipped his head back and gritted his teeth.

Kaylee answered for him. "Blayne is ready for some pain medication."

"Okay. I'll let his nurse know."

Kaylee rubbed his forehead until the nurse came in a few minutes later with a syringe. She hooked it to the IV line and Blayne put his hand on her arm and said, "What are you giving me?"

"Ketorolac."

"Not a narcotic?"

"No. This is what the doctor ordered."

Blayne nodded once and dropped his hand. The nurse pushed the medication slowly into his IV then said. "That should start working right away."

"Good," he said to Kaylee as the nurse left. "I need to go see Mama C."

After ten minutes, the grimace on his face only eased slightly, though. "Blayne, maybe you should let them give you something a little stronger." Kaylee couldn't stand to see him sweating with pain, his eyes screwed shut.

"No," he said harshly. Then softer, "No. I can't risk it, Kay. I'll be fine."

Several minutes later he opened his eyes. "Well, I think this is as good as it's gonna get. Let's go see Mama."

"Let me get a wheelchair." Kaylee hurried out before he could protest.

The nurse came in and unhooked his IV and helped him into the wheelchair. Sweat dripped from his forehead and he gritted his teeth, his jaw muscles flexing with the effort. "Give me a sec," he said, panting.

"I can ask the doctor for something stronger," the nurse said, her brows knit together.

"No." He laid his head in his hand. "I can't. I'm a drug addict."

"Recovering," Kaylee added.

The nurse nodded in understanding. "Well, when you get back, I have a couple of non-pharmaceutical things we can try."

The trip to MICU would have been comical if not for Blayne's pain. Pushing a wheelchair with one hand was not an easy task. Especially with someone as big as Blayne sitting in it.

In Mama C's room, Blayne gripped her hand, tears rolling freely from his eyes. "Mama, please. Why are you just giving up?"

She'd given him the same spiel she'd given Kaylee—about wanting to be with her husband and son.

"It's just my time," she whispered, unable to speak any louder.

"But what about the others?" Blayne begged. "Hannah and Clint and DeMarcus. They need you."

A faint smile crept onto Mama's face and she laid a hand on Kaylee's and squeezed Blayne's. "They don't need me anymore. They have you two now."

Blayne looked up at Kaylee. The sorrow in his eyes almost too much to bear.

Mama C continued. "I want you two to send them home. Help them get home. Those children need their real mamas." She turned her steel gaze to Blayne. "And you. It's time for you to call your mama. You're ready. Kaylee will be there for you."

KAYLEE'S PARENTS took her to her apartment to change clothes and grab a toothbrush then they dropped her off at the hospital on their way to their hotel. She spent the night in the chair next to Blayne's bed even though he protested, telling her to go home and sleep in her own bed. Neither of them got much sleep, Blayne's pain kept them both up. Even with an ice pack and repositioning, the medication barely took the edge off.

The doctor rounded on him in the morning and said he could be discharged. Kaylee picked up his prescriptions and had her parents pick up a pair of jeans and a stretchy t-shirt for him. She really was glad they'd come. She didn't know what she'd do without them since her car was still impounded as part of the investigation.

Kaylee's parents sat in the waiting room, anxious to meet this man their daughter confessed to being in love with. She took the clothes in to him. He was sitting in a chair by the bed, his face still screwed up in a tight grimace. "Where did you get those?" he asked.

"My, um, my parents went and got them for you. They're, uh, waiting out there to meet you."

His eyes widened like a schoolboy caught cheating. "What am I going to say to them?"

"I don't know. Hello, maybe?" She smiled.

"But I...I almost got you killed. They," he swallowed, "aren't they furious with me? Don't they hate—"

Kaylee quieted him by kissing him softly. When she pulled away, she said, "They are excited to meet you. And very thankful that you saved my life."

"Do that again."

She turned her head and raised an eyebrow. "What?"

He attempted to smile. "Kiss me. I think that works better for the pain than the medication does."

She laughed and shook her head. She bent over and he pulled her into his lap. They kissed with a gentle touch, their lips brushing softly against one another. Kaylee leaned in to deepen it, then pulled back. "Ouch." She touched her swollen, split lip. "Better keep it soft for now."

Before Blayne could protest, she was moving her lips across his again, only stopping when the door opened. "Oh, umm," Kaylee struggled to stand. "We were just..."

The nurse smiled. "Oh, I know what you were just doing. Your discharge papers are signed. I see you have some clothes to change into." She turned to Kaylee. "Do you want to help him change?"

Kaylee's face flushed. "No. We aren't...we haven't...I mean. No. I'll wait outside." She chanced a glance at Blayne and blushed even harder at the glint in his eyes.

Laughing, the nurse said, "Okay, how about I help him with his pants, but you come back in so I can show you the easiest way to put his shirt on. It looks like you might need to know this for yourself, too." She gestured at Kaylee's sling.

"Yeah, okay." Kaylee slipped out the door and tried to fan the redness out of her face and neck with her hand.

When the nurse called for her to come back in, Blayne's face was pale and covered in sweat again. He leaned on the bed, panting. "Give me just a minute."

Kaylee realized her mouth hung open, and she shut it. Blayne without a shirt—even pale, sweating Blayne with a big dressing on his chest, without a shirt—was astounding. How could someone who'd been homeless for three years, have such great abs? And pecs. And biceps. And everything. Kaylee shook her head and diverted her eyes. The nurse appeared to be amused by her gawking and Kaylee's face blossomed into flames again.

"Okay," Blayne breathed. "Let's do this." He looked up at Kaylee then at the nurse. "What?"

"Nothing," they both said.

The nurse talked Kaylee through helping him put his shirt on, then the sling and swath. She went through the discharge instructions, including how to care for his wound and when to follow up, with both of them. Blayne signed the papers, and they were ready to go.

He hesitated at the door. "I'm a little nervous. About meeting your family."

"Well, hopefully you can repay the favor soon, when I finally get to meet your parents."

Blayne grunted.

They walked slowly, Blayne still weak from his near-death experience. The only reason the nurse hadn't insisted on a wheelchair for his discharge was because they weren't actually leaving the hospital. Kaylee's family stood when they entered the waiting room. Her dad stepped forward and extended his hand. As they shook hands, he said, "Blayne, it's so nice to meet you. My name is Clarence." He paused and looked down. When he spoke again, he choked up. "Thank you for saving her life."

Blayne replied. "It's a pleasure to meet you, sir." He glanced at Kaylee then back at her dad. "I would die to protect your daughter."

Kaylee's mom, crying, stepped between him and Clarence wrapped her arms around him. "Thank you," she blubbered.

Blayne froze, looking flustered for a moment. Then he put his right arm around her and let her cry, not pulling away until she did, his own eyes filled with tears.

Kaylee's mom wiped her face and cleared her throat. "I'm Linda. And you are every bit as handsome as Kaylee said you were."

"Mom!" Kaylee, of course, blushed.

"Well, he is." Linda winked at Blayne.

"Hey, guys," Luke said, stepping into the circle. "I think we should let these two sit down. Blayne looks pretty pale." He looked at Blayne. "I'm Luke. The awesome little brother."

"Nice to meet you, Luke," Blayne said. "And, from everything your sister has told me about you, you truly are awesome. And a bit spoiled."

Luke smirked and shrugged. "What can I say? Some people deserve to be spoiled." He took Blayne by the right arm and led him toward a chair. "Now sit down before you fall down."

Sweat sprung out on Blayne's forehead and upper lip again as he gingerly sat.

Linda, concern etched into the creases in her face, said, "Are you sure they didn't release you too soon?"

Blayne looked at Kaylee and nodded, giving her permission to speak for him.

She laid her hand on his knee. "Blayne is having a hard time with pain control. He's a recovering drug addict and refuses to take narcotics."

Luke was first to speak. "Wow, dude, that's badass."

"Luke! Language," Linda said. "But, indeed, that is badass."

Everyone laughed.

"That takes a lot of grit, young man," Clarence said. "I don't know that I'd be able to do that. Even with the strong stuff, I was a huge baby after my ankle surgery."

Kaylee's mom nodded.

"You guys...you aren't gonna judge me?" Blayne said in wonder.

"No, son," Kaylee's dad said softly. "We all have things we'd rather not remember from our past. It's what you do from here on that matters."

Blayne shook his head. "But my past life got your daughter kidnapped. She could have been killed because of me."

Clarence scooted his chair, positioning it directly in front of Blayne. He leaned in, his gaze never leaving Blayne's eyes. "You can't control the actions of others, Blayne, just your own. And your actions were heroic."

CHAPTER 27

"Your family is amazing," Blayne said.

"Yeah, they really are." Kaylee smiled even though she was struggling to push the wheelchair she'd "borrowed" to get Blayne to Mama C's room.

Mama C had been moved to a hospice room on the regular medical floor. She'd refused all treatment, including antibiotics, fluids, and breathing treatments. She was only allowing oxygen, the nurse had told them, because she wanted to be alert for their visit.

As hard as it was, they had agreed to each other that they would honor Mama C's wishes and vowed that neither of them would leave her side until it was over.

The room was larger and much quieter than her room in the MICU had been. Kaylee parked Blayne on one side of the bed and she went to the other side.

Mama C started right in. "I want you two to do me a favor."

"Of course," Kaylee answered.

"I wanna see the others. The kids. Before I go."

Just saying those few words seemed to take all she had. She closed her eyes, her chest rattled with each laborious breath she drew.

Kaylee and Blayne looked at each other over her bed, her shell of a body. Neither of them wanted to leave her side, but they'd known this request was coming. They'd talked about it that morning. Kaylee whispered, "I'll call Allie."

Blayne nodded.

She took her phone over by the window and Facetimed her

friend. "Allie," she said, making sure the camera was positioned to catch the movement of her lips. "I have a huge favor to ask of you."

Allie rolled her eyes. "It seems like there have been a lot of those lately. Ask away."

Kaylee explained the situation and asked Allie if she would drive down to the viaduct and see if the three kids were there. She'd met them when Max had gone down to examine Mama C, and they should all be able to recognize her. If any of them were there, Allie would bring them to the hospital. If not, she would call back. Allie agreed, not even ending with a smart-aleck remark.

Sighing, Kaylee went back to Mama C's bedside and laid her hand on the woman's arm. Blayne looked up at her expectantly and she nodded, lips pursed against her emotions.

"Mama?" Kaylee said. "I have someone who'd like to talk to you on the phone."

Sick as she was, Mama C was still able to open her eyes and give a look that made Kaylee's knees quake. "And who might that be?"

"Don't be mad at me, please," Kaylee pleaded. "But I got in contact with your old friends in New York. Beth wants to talk to you."

"Beth?" Mama C whispered. A tear struggled crookedly down her cheek, following the lines of wrinkles.

Kaylee nodded and called Beth's number. As it rang, she held the phone to Mama's ear.

"Oh Beth," Mama croaked out, "it's been so long." A weak cough followed her inhalation of breath.

The only other words Mama spoke during the call were, "I'm sorry. I was so broken...*am* so broken."

An hour passed before Kaylee's phone buzzed with Allie's text: *On our way.* Mama C hadn't even opened her eyes again during that time. All Kaylee and Blayne could do was look at each other hopelessly.

Allie knocked before entering, then went straight to where Kaylee sat next to the bed and put her hands on her friend's shoulders. DeMarcus, Hannah, and Clint followed her in, more subdued than Kaylee had ever seen them. Dirty tear streaks painted Hannah's face like rain running down a grimy window. Kaylee moved out of the way and the three of them stood together across from Blayne, looking down at Mama C.

Blayne touched her face and said, "Mama, they're here."

She opened her eyes and looked first at him, then at the three devastated teens. Her cracked lips attempted a smile.

Hannah sobbed, "Mama, we didn't know where you went. We went to try to find Blayne, and you were gone when we got back."

Mama C moved her hand toward the girl, too weak to lift it.

"Hold her hand, Hannah," Blayne said in a library tone. Or a funeral tone.

She did, still sobbing.

"It's okay child. My turn to talk." She closed her eyes and struggled against her diseased lungs to draw in enough breath to continue. "You all," she looked at each of them in turn, "need to go home. Home to your real mamas."

DeMarcus shook his head and wiped his face with the back of his hands.

Mama pinned him with a look. "You have family. Go to them."

She closed her eyes again. This time it took her much longer to get enough breath. "Kaylee, tell them."

Kaylee glanced at Blayne, and he nodded. She took a breath before speaking. "Blayne and I will help you contact your families."

DeMarcus shook his head again and cleared his throat.

Kaylee continued before he could speak. "DeMarcus, you don't have to go back to your dad. Who else could you go to, to get you off the streets?"

He looked down, his face twisted with anguish. "My nana. She'll take me in."

"Why didn't you just go to her to begin with?" Blayne asked.

The young boy shrugged. "I didn't want her to have to deal with my dad. She doesn't need that."

"That's her choice to make, Dee," Blayne said.

They talked quietly about who each of them could call and left Kaylee with a small list of numbers to find. Allie hugged her before leaving to take the kids to the shelter, where Blayne and Kaylee promised to find them after Mama passed.

The last thing Mama C said to them was, "Take care of each other. Don't let Blayne get in trouble, college girl. Love wins. Love always wins." She closed her eyes then, only to open them one last time around two in the morning as she drew her last breath. She stared at the foot of her bed, a look of joyous recognition on her face. She reached a hand up, then dropped it, closing her eyes with a smile.

CHAPTER 28

The sun shone from a clear sky. Spring was close; Kaylee could smell it in the air. Blayne held tight to her hand, chewing at the inside of his cheeks.

In an attempt to calm his anxiety, she stopped walking and pulled him around to face her. She cupped his face and smiled when his ocean-blue eyes locked on hers. Then she kissed him as if no one else existed on the busy sidewalk. The short kiss lit a fire in her belly, and when she pulled away, Blayne's eyes remained closed. He pulled her close and sighed.

When he released her and grabbed her hand again, she said, "Ready?"

He nodded.

They entered the restaurant and looked around. A young girl, around ten-years-old, bounced up and down on the balls of her feet. As soon as she spotted Blayne, she squealed and rushed to him, skidding to a stop and throwing her arms around him. She choked out, "Blayne." And then she cried as he held her close. Blayne had opened up to Kaylee just recently about what had caused him to leave home. He'd told her before that he'd almost killed his little sister, but no specifics. In a rough voice and with moist eyes he'd recounted the events: he'd had several sheets of stickers laced with hallucinogenic drugs sitting on his nightstand in anticipation of a rave he was planning to sneak out to that night. Seven-year-old Lizzy had found them and plastered about six of them on her bare arms before he caught her. She'd almost died on the way to the ER, then twice again before they could get her stabilized. He'd left that next morning, after news that she would be okay.

Kaylee stepped out of the way as his parents closed in, embracing both of their children for the first time in years.

"Kaylee, get over here," his dad's voice was gruff as he opened the embrace to invite her in.

"Uh, your table is ready," the hostess said. Kaylee could tell she didn't want to interrupt, but there were people waiting behind them.

The group followed her, winding through the restaurant. Blayne kept his arm around his sister's shoulders. He ruffled her hair. "Lizzy, you've grown."

"Yeah. That happens in three years." She rolled her eyes, but the smile on her face beamed like sunshine at noon on the Fourth of July.

They'd all spoken on the phone multiple times since Mama C's death, but this was the first time Blayne's family had been able to come to Denver. After they finished eating, they sat around the table, talking.

"How's your job going?" Blayne's mom asked him.

"Great. I love it. Kelly, she's the supervisor, had me helping her with paperwork and stuff while my collarbone healed, and she said I'd make a great project manager some day. So, the company is going to pay for me to take some online classes." Blayne's eyes sparkled.

"And, what about you Kaylee? What are your plans after graduation?"

Blayne squeezed her hand and looked down at her with a smile.

"Oh, I have a job lined up at one of the Denver area homeless shelters. I'm going to help get people, young people in particular, off the streets."

Blayne added, "She already has all the paperwork in to start a charity fund called 'Mama C's Kids'—the owners of the local sports teams and some of the players have already pledged huge amounts of money to get it started."

"That's amazing." Blayne's mom teared up again. "Though I expect nothing less from you, Kaylee."

"Thank you. It's important to me." She glanced up at Blayne.

"The big question is," his dad said, "what's the plan with you two?"

"I think the plan should be marriage," Lizzy piped up. "Can I be a bridesmaid?"

And of course, heat rose up Kaylee's neck and face.

Blayne just laughed and put his arm around Kaylee, pulling her closer to his side. "Yes, Lizzy, I'm sure Kaylee will let you be a bridesmaid when the time comes."

ABOUT THE AUTHOR

Holli Anderson has a Bachelor's Degree in Nursing—which has nothing to do with writing, except maybe by adding some pretty descriptive injury and vomit scenes to her books. She discovered her joy of writing during a very trying period in her life when escaping into make-believe saved her. She enjoys reading any book she gets her hands on.

Along with her husband, Steve, and their four sons, she lives in Grantsville, Utah—the same small town in which she grew up.

This has been an
Immortal Production

CPSIA information can be obtained
at www.ICGtesting.com
Printed in the USA
LVHW032148140421
684525LV00011B/539